The Spilled Potion

WITHDRAWN

MISHAL IMAAN SYED

W9-CLY-734

ISBN-10: 1494276968
ISBN-13: 9781494276966
Library of Congress Control Number: 2013921806
CreateSpace Independent Publishing Platform
North Charleston, South Carolina

Part I

One

Temper Tantrum

If you think about how exasperating my sister was being on that morning, you'll realize that I meant no harm when I turned her into a sweet little bunny.

It all began one day when Mom came in to wake me up for school. I was drowsy, having stayed up late the previous night reading a book, and in no mood to be awakened. Mom was just beginning to get annoyed with me when my highly aggravating little sister, Allie, pranced in and announced that she had a bad headache and could she please, please, *please* stay home from school?

Mom frowned. I could tell she knew that my little sister, a pesky third grader, was scheming something. She whisked Allie down into the kitchen and told me to be ready for breakfast in fifteen minutes. Snuggling back down cozily, I reminded myself not to go back to sleep. At least not if I could help it.

Suddenly, I remembered that my book report on *Moby Dick* was not ready. Yikes! I'd worked on it assiduously last night, but my last paragraph still wasn't done.

I sprang out of bed and *flew*—literally—down the stairs to brush my teeth.

Now, I have to tell you a little bit about my family. We're a bit, you might say, *special.* That's because everyone in my family is a witch or a wizard.

Don't get me wrong, we don't mutter nonsensical "magic words" over boiling pots of steaming potions. We don't threaten to turn people into black beetles or three-headed toads. In fact, we do pretty much everything the same way normal people do, except for a few things like doing the dishes and cooking. Still, we like to keep our identities secret—it's better than having a whole lot of *normal* people following us around wanting all of their problems solved by magic. Nobody in my family looks very eccentric (well, except for my hair...I'll explain that later). My sister, Allie, is very chubby and cute besides being annoying, although I must say I could do without that last feature. My parents like to blend in and take on normal jobs like teaching mythology part time at a local university (my mom) and working for a telecom company (my dad) instead of taking on witchy labor such as domesticating unicorns. We even live in a normal house in a normal town, which is Sioux Falls, South Dakota.

I'm not sure about the rest of my family, but using magic usually gets me out of quite a lot of trouble. Oh, and it also gets me into some. Like how it did that day.

This particular morning, my sister had decided to be unusually difficult. When I came out of the bathroom, I heard Mom telling her that her temperature was fine and that if she was really sick her forehead would be hot. My cheeks felt warm with suppressed laughter. I had tried the same trick more than a few times when I was younger and had long since realized that it yielded disastrous results. But Allie did not stop there. Instead, she turned herself into an orange and sat calmly in the fruit bowl so that it took us forever to figure out which one she was. Then, she turned herself into a bird and almost flew out of the window. After that, she argued endlessly with Mom about her not feeling well and claimed that if Mom cared about her, she would let her stay home from school.

After a while, I heard a door slam. Allie had locked herself in the bathroom upstairs. When she came out, her face was bright red and sweaty. I wondered what she was up to now.

She marched right up to Mom and told her to check her temperature again. Mom did, and to my astonishment, it was actually higher! Mom gave in, and Allie got to stay home. I wish I had been smart enough to figure out something like what Allie had done when I was in third grade.

I was nearly late for school, but I got there just in time. As you can imagine, I hadn't had time to finish the report that morning, so I stammered and tried to make something up for the last paragraph.

When I was finished with my presentation, I handed my report to Ms. Davidson and stood there apprehensively while she looked it over, hoping that she wouldn't examine the end too closely. She raised her eyes from the page and looked straight at me. I squirmed under her harsh gaze.

"Zoey," she said, sounding sort of tired, as if I *never* turn anything in on time, "this report looks as if it is incomplete. Where is your last paragraph, in which you were supposed to talk about which portion of the story interests you most?"

I sighed. Why oh why couldn't she tell me this in private instead of with the whole class staring, amused, at me? And what a boring, strenuous novel to have to read! I was beginning to wonder if I should turn Ms. Davidson into an ant for a few minutes or so.

But I had to say something, so I lied sheepishly, "Um, Ms. Davidson, I think the last paragraph was on a separate page. I must have forgotten to print it out."

"Hmm," she said. "Well, Zoey, since you have forgotten a portion of your report at home, you will have to complete an extra portion from the whale's point of view, to be turned in tomorrow along with the missing portion of your report."

OK, fine with me, as long as I didn't get a bad grade. But would she please stop using the annoying word *portion*!

At the end of the day, Ms. Davidson called on me and said I needed to go to the front office. Apparently, my sister would be waiting there. I grinned to myself. Allie must have been found out and delivered to school late after all. I would be walking home with her.

When we got home, I found a Post-it note stuck on the door.

Zoey ~ Will be late home. Forgot to tell you this morning. Big meeting. Have your homework done before I get home. ~ Mom

Oh, so that's why Allie was sent to school today. But I'd known that Mom had her doubts about Allie being truly sick all along.

4

The door was unlocked. I pushed it open and sat Allie firmly down on the sofa.

"Allie, sit here and watch whatever you want on TV…*Shake it Up* or something. I have to do my homework. I have lots of it today, and I don't want you disturbing me."

She is most definitely *not* allowed to watch *Shake it Up*, but it was the only way to deal with her. I opened the fridge and got out chocolate chip cookies, orange juice, and grapes. After giving them to Allie, I decided I might as well start my homework. I went to a part of the house where noise from the television set wouldn't bother me and began doing long, strenuous pages of algebra equations.

Two

The Failed Frog Incantation

Anyway, when I was finally finished with *that* part of my homework (my teacher does not believe in giving kids free time), I was struck by the quietness in the house. It seemed so empty. I tiptoed to the living room and saw that the TV had been turned off. Darn it! Why couldn't Allie leave me a moment's peace? I went upstairs into my room to look for her and then froze.

My *entire room* had been turned upside down. Drawers were pulled out, their contents strewn all over the place. Melted crayons left gigantic stains on my peach-colored carpet. Threads had been pulled out of my favorite aqua rug. Some of Allie's stuffed animals only added to the horrendous mess.

Worst of all, a few pieces from my mini glass animal collection were broken. I could have thrown Allie out the window. It is easy enough to zap a few things back into their original places when you're a thirteen-year-old witch, but a mess this big…well, just use your imagination. I began to meditate on all sorts of dire punishments for that girl.

I couldn't find my infuriating little sister anywhere, though I badly wanted to give her a piece of my mind. I looked in her room, in the master bedroom, in the guestroom, in the kitchen, in every single bathroom—even in the attic, where the lingering odor of rats fairly overwhelmed me. Unfortunately, she was nowhere to be found.

By now I had gotten very worried. My anger had almost all diminished, and I couldn't imagine where Allie had gone. What if she had been kidnapped? As much as I hated her right then, I didn't want her to get killed. What if I never found her? What if a burglar was at fault here and not my little sister at all? What if she had run away without me knowing? What if this and what if that. I was so caught up with my ridiculous, outrageous, incredibly farfetched what-if questions I couldn't think straight. It occurred to me then that I hadn't realized the obvious. I darted outside into the front yard. No Allie to be seen there. But what about the back? To my dismay, I had no luck there either. I ran out to a secluded corner of our property, which extends to a ten-foot radius of wooded area, and then I saw her.

She was sitting on a plastic folding chair with a large book in her lap. The book had leather covers, heavy with mud, and its pages were badly torn. Allie seemed intently focused on the book, something which I had never seen her do before. Allie didn't even seem to notice that I was watching. In front of her, on a little wooden table which I was surprised she was strong enough to drag out, sat a cage with a mini pond and rocks in it. When I looked closer, I saw that it was occupied by her spotted pet frog, Lilly.

I could feel my rage coming back to me again. I no longer felt sorry for and worried about my little sister. It was clear that she had caused the damage. I was merely confused and very, *very* angry.

I marched right up to Allie, and she looked up at me, startled. I could see fear take hold of her small features as she saw my state. She decided to make her eyes big and innocent looking. I hate it when she does that. Puppy eyes are my specialty, not hers.

"Allison Mariah Williams," I said sternly, "what are you doing here? And why did you mess up my room?"

My sister looked up at me blankly. She didn't say anything.

"Oh, well, if you're not going to admit, then I'm telling Mom how you *'borrowed'* her favorite raspberry-flavored lipstick, shared it with your measly little friends over the weekend, and then took it to school last week," I snapped.

Realizing the seriousness of the situation, she muttered, "I wasn't doing anything wrong. My spell went wrong, that's all."

Yeah, right.

"What spell?" I asked suspiciously.

"I was trying to turn Lilly into a puppy. I like puppies better than frogs," Allie explained sweetly. I could tell from her expression she was telling the truth. But I felt a pang of sorrow for Lilly. Was it possible for a frog to get dizzy? Then I heard Allie's high-pitched whining, and I snapped back to the present.

"Oh, Zoey, it was an accident! Please believe me! It wasn't my fault! It was Lilly's fault! She said she thought golden, fuzzy, teddy bear breed puppies were cute, so she said that she wanted to be one. I didn't do anything, I swear!" She pushed her neon-pink-and-blue hair out of her face.

"Yeah, I'm sure you didn't do anything. Well, if *didn't do anything* means turning my room into a tornado zone, making me search through the house for you, getting me worried sick, torturing your innocent pet frog, and possibly making me late for yet *another* homework assignment," I grumbled sarcastically.

"I told you already, it was Lilly's fault!"

"First of all, frogs can't talk. Second of all, you shouldn't be messing around with spells you know you're too young to be doing. And third of all, clear off to your room *right now* and don't get into any more TROUBLE!" I cried.

"I can clean it up for you," Allie protested feebly, but by the look on my face she knew that she shouldn't say anything more.

Hoping Allie would behave and thinking about how I could punish her, I wandered back into the house, down the main hall, and to my parents' bedroom. I smiled as I smelled the enticing lavender vanilla-scented air and gazed dreamily at the tan fleur-de-lis wallpaper. It was refreshing, but I had business to take care of in there before Mom got home.

The old cherry-colored bookshelf stood tall in the far corner of the room, weathered with bumps and scratches. After dragging over a stool to stand on, I pulled down a leather-bound general reference witchery volume from the set of witchcraft encyclopedias. I blew the dust softly off its cover and set it delicately on my parents' fancy dove quilt (EXTREMELY old-fashioned!). I had to work quickly to finish this appalling task off before Mom came home.

I carefully turned the yellowed pages until I found the passage I was looking for, written in elegant script. Mom had shown it to me a few weeks ago during my Witchcraft lessons.

When faced with a difficult situation involving a displaced object or displaced objects, a witch or wizard must transfer his/her inner power to the object or objects concerned. To do this, one must dose the object or objects with an incantation involving several actions and humming as to return them to their rightful locations. The formula is as follows:
Clap one's hands twice loudly, begin to hum softly and reach a crescendo point within a relatively minimal time window, whistle once for six beats, and clap one's hands together again three times.

Um. What? It took me a few times reading the paragraph through, but eventually I was able to decipher what it meant. I gulped as I realized I couldn't whistle.

I tried to whistle loud enough, but it sounded more like a tortured wolf howling under a full moon. I tried again with the same results. This was going to take longer than I thought.

Three

A Little Bit of Magic

I lay on my back on my frilly pink bed, utterly exhausted. After lots of false starts, grunts, hums, whistling, claps, grunting, and groaning, I had finally succeeded in getting my room back in shape. Best of all, I had told on Allie, and there she was downstairs getting yelled at and preached at by Mom. Never had I been happier to see my little sister in trouble.

The next day after school, Mom was home. Fortunately Allie would be under her supervision the *entire* afternoon so I could have time to complete my overdue homework assignment. Yes, Ms. Davidson did assign me extra make-up work because my work was overdue, but Mom had e-mailed her to say that there had been a "little incident" at my house and that I would complete the assignment today. It had kept me from having to do extra homework. That was definitely one thing I could be grateful to Mom for. No, make that two, if you count lecturing my highly despicable little sister.

Later, at about half past four that afternoon, I heard frustrated grunts coming from the kitchen. The kitchen door was closed, so I tiptoed silently up to it, pressed my ear against it, and listened. Allie was in there with Mom. Little snippets of conversation drifted out from inside.

"Yes, I understand, Allie…Be good…Tell your sister…I expect a good report…Your behavior yesterday was appalling…Don't argue with me…No, I will be back sooner than that."

Oh no! Was Mom going somewhere? That would leave me Allie to contend with by myself. Hopefully Mom's little lecture had done her some good.

The kitchen door opened. I ducked behind the sofa just in time. Then I heard Mom calling my name.

"Zoey! Zoey," she yelled up the stairs. "I just remembered I'd forgotten some stuff—just some milk cartons—when I went grocery shopping on Saturday, so I want you to take care of Allison. And I also want to get something for your cousins, who will be coming this weekend. Haute Couture isn't very far, so I'll be back soon enough to cook dinner. Please take care of Allie and give her something to do. She'll be good! Bye!"

And just like that, she disappeared out the front door. Now, you might be wondering why we witches and wizards don't simply magically transport ourselves wherever we want to go. That's only because anyone who witnesses a witch spontaneously emerging from thin air will run screaming out the door (or something like that, because…well…you know what I mean.)

As soon as Mom left, I came out from behind the sofa and found Allie sitting on it, staring hard at the blank TV. I wondered why she hadn't turned it on.

As if reading my thoughts, Allie enlightened me about the situation. "I cast a dancing spell on Dad last week and he couldn't stop tap dancing for an hour, so

I can't watch TV for two weeks. Mom said to tell you. She's so mean, isn't she?!"

"C'mon!" I exclaimed cheerfully, a sudden idea popping into my head. "We're going to perform a spell." And before Allie could respond, she was being dragged violently up the stairs and into my room.

"Ow, that hurt. You shouldn't have done that," Allie admonished bitterly.

"Whatever. Now get me my spell book so we can begin this. Act like the good little girl I haven't been seeing much of lately."

"Are you implying that I'm not a good girl?"

"No, I'm *stating* that you're not a good girl."

"That's so mean!"

"As I said, get me the book right now or we won't get to have the spell. Effective immediately," I added hastily.

Allie shot me a look of distaste and bolted down the stairs. That was one of the pros of being a big sister, I thought. Your younger sibling just had to do things for you when you asked them to......or else their good-little-girl façade after stealing Mom's Raspberry Glitterati lipstick would be discovered and fixed in a rather harsh manner.

Soon, after thoroughly examining my parents' bookshelf to find the book, Allie trotted into my room carrying a slightly newer, paperback textbook with color illustrations. It was a modernized specimen of what Mom calls my "Witchiness Practice Books," and its text was (thankfully) a great deal more understandable than the text of the book I'd read earlier.

Allie looked at me questioningly as I flipped rapidly through its bright white pages, not bothering to look at the table of contents. A mischievous grin spread over my face as I realized that I might be able to cast a spell on my little sister. Not a truly *bad* spell, of course, but still something interesting. Maybe I could turn her into a dolphin…or a kitten…or a sweet puppy…even a bunny. The possibilities were endless. Of course, I'd have to check out how to turn her back into a human as well, since I don't want to have an animal for a sister (or maybe I do, and if I do, it's completely Allie's fault!).

At last I found the page I was looking for. Apparently, there was a potion required to morph a human into a domestic animal, but as I read down the list of ingredients, it turned out that they were all basic household/kitchen substances, except for one of them. I had never done a morphing spell using potion before, so this was going to be a challenge for me.

Allie looked over my shoulder at the book. "Who are you turning into a bunny?" she asked curiously.

I grinned uneasily. "Um, Allie? Would *you* like to be turned into a bunny? Just for a while, I promise. And I'll make you into a cute bunny. I'll have to change you back before Mom comes home, of course. But you can't tell *anyone*. Mom or Dad or Kiera or Nikki or our other cousins or *anyone*. You have to keep spells a secret, OK?"

"'Kay," Allie said brightly. "I promise. But can I tell the goldfish?"

"Allie, you seriously need help, and I don't mean that in a kind or concerned manner. Because I can assure you, animals are both mentally and physically incapable of—"

"Fine! I get it! And can we start already?!"

"Now we have to go into the kitchen. Don't mess around with Mom's stuff there, and be absolutely quiet. Stay still while I perform the spell, and whatever you do, *don't talk.* If you say something dumb or idiotic, it can turn the spell upside-down, and you can be stuck in bunny state forever!"

Allie covered her mouth with her baby-chubby hands (which I noticed had been sloppily manicured using MY makeup and were still not dry), pretending to be shocked, dismayed, and overly satisfied all at once. "Oooh, you said a bad word! Two of them!" she grinned. She covered her face with her hands in a look of mock shock, streaking her forehead with nail polish.

"Allie!" I moaned, "you're in third grade, and you *still* think that 'dumb' and 'idiotic' are bad words! Get over that, seriously! Grow up!"

In the kitchen, I opened cupboard after cupboard in search of the ingredients for the potion. Mom had conveniently left next Saturday's grocery list on the fridge, and none of the materials for the potion were on the list. This meant that we had all those ingredients at home.

Of course, each potion that a witch or a wizard creates has at least one additional special ingredient. My parents have this drawer labeled "extra potion ingredients," which they use whenever they're experimenting with potions. My potion required one ounce of ground dragon talons—gross! As I dug through the drawer, I found the craziest things, such as "shredded Pegasus wings" and "freeze-dried unicorn silk." I tried to memorize the ingredients of the potion as I made it, in case I ever needed it again.

After I created the potion, I'd have to perform some special spells in order to make the potion actually work. You can't just mix ranch dressing, dragon talons, and vinegar and turn someone into a bunny.

And even if you do, you have to have the original potion you made to turn them back again.

I was still searching for the ingredients I needed when I noticed a magic teapot-shaped, protruding ledge behind the coffeemaker. Surprised, I pushed the machine out of the way and pulled the handle or ledge or whatever it was outward. Nothing budged. I tried again, this time pushing it. It *still* didn't move. I tried a third time, pulling it outward and then upward. I was amazed when it actually opened.

Inside that cupboard-like thing was a seemingly ordinary-looking shelf with a hawk carved in it. The shelf was empty, which was why I could actually see the hawk. But when you pulled its handle outward, there was *another* shelf behind it, filled with the most bizarre things!

I sneezed when I opened the hidden cupboard. Stacked on the first stone ledge were small note-books of different shapes and sizes, musty and dusty. I guiltily opened one and saw that it was filled with random sentences written in what looked like code— a mishmash of numbers, capital letters, and small symbols. There was no name on the entry, but it was dated 1948. I had no time to look at the notebooks further, so I scanned down the next ledge. Here, there were glass bottles and vials of random, unrecognizable liquids. And some of them were in colors I had NEVER SEEN BEFORE! *Oh my gosh*, I thought excitedly, *I didn't know witches and wizards could see past the human spectrum!* Sometimes I wonder if we're a different species altogether. I moved on to the next ledge before I noticed that Allie was sitting on a wooden chair quietly in the corner, being good of her own accord. Hmm…what a change!

Here, there were more random bottles and vials, only this time most of them had labels. *Potion to turn someone into a kitten…potion to torture your teacher…potion to create super-sticky raspberry-flavored mint gum* (does that even make sense?)…*potion to feed your enemies…BEWARE, potion to turn someone into a mutant alien.* I laughed when I read the last two. I wondered what a mutant alien looked like. And those were only a few of the numerous labels…

On the next and last ledge, there were older, leather-bound spell books similar to the ones that my parents had on their bookshelf. I opened one and my eye fell on a diagram of how to create your own duplicate. I should try that sometime. It would come in handy if I didn't feel like going to school, which was often—or more appropriately, whenever I had math class, which was every day.

After examining the book more closely and not finding much of interest, I slammed it shut. Immediately a billowing cloud of thick dust rose up into the air. I sneezed violently. Allie had an even worse sneezing fit. She simply couldn't stop her sneezing, and she fell to her knees on the linoleum-tiled kitchen floor. I gasped as she flipped and did a triple summersault in mid-air. It's a little-known fact that witches and wizards are prone to do such abnormally acrobatic things when irked badly. Howling like she'd just been kidnapped by a band of outlaws, all with contagious bronchitis, Allie began to perform amazing aerial stunts with her small body. This went on for a while and didn't cease even for one moment.

Um, someone come help?

Eventually Allie must have gotten tired of her sneezing, and landed on the ground with a thud. She looked bewildered for a second and then started to whimper. For once I felt sorry for her.

I picked the fallen book up off the ground and began the ordeal of shoving it back in place on the crammed shelf when I noticed something mildly interesting.

On the third shelf, above this one, there was a little bottle with some sort of glittery blue potion in it. It was right in the front row of bottles, and I could've sworn it hadn't been there a minute ago.

I was used to this kind of thing, being a witch, but there was something different about this potion. I picked up the heavy, thick glass bottle and there was one thing I realized at once. This container was *perfectly ordinary.* There was nothing weird about it— except for the mysterious substance in it, of course. It was just a regular old *bottle.*

I turned it over in my fingers, wondering why there wasn't a label on it, when I saw the compressed black printing on the opposite side.

POTION TO TURN SOMEONE INTO A BUNNY

Gulp.

Um, wasn't that the exact potion I'd been wishing for a moment ago?

I can't really explain what I did next. I knew by extensively studying witch etiquette that I should never use an unknown or suspicious concoction on anyone without permission and research. Maybe I was just too excited by my discovery, maybe I was too freaked out about the mysterious potion that had spontaneously *appeared* on the shelf, or maybe I just wasn't thinking…but either way, what I did just then I would regret for weeks afterward.

I ordered Allie to stand still and not say a word. With trembling hands, I poured a minute droplet of the magic substance into her open mouth.

There was a blinding flash of bright white light, then the temperature in the room shifted from super hot to ice cold, making me shiver. Suddenly everything went absolutely black.

Four

My Gigantic Lie...Someone's Hiding a

Dirty Little Secret

I don't remember clearly what happened after that—from that moment to the time Mom came home. All I remember is this:

When I woke up, everything appeared to be the same. Nothing in the kitchen was out of place. A UFO with deranged aliens on board hadn't suddenly appeared smack in the middle of our living room floor. (Thank goodness for that. Considering the flustered state that I was in, I really can't be held responsible for what I'd do.) But something was missing from the scene.

That something was Allie. She had completely disappeared, which was not surprising, taking into consideration that when I looked down, I saw—*poof*—a little goldenish-brown bunny with an adorable face and a creamy-white tail at my feet.

The bunny, I mean Allie, was very cute. She had soft, puffy ears; fuzzy, golden paws; and a tail that felt like it was made out of a pom-pom. I stroked her, and she whimpered softly.

My heart melted. Even in her human form, I had never seen my sister look so adorable before—which was saying something.

This was before I noticed the broken glass and sparkly potion seeping into the tiled floor. The air around it was sort of shimmery.

But I hadn't thought about the consequences of my actions. I remembered reading somewhere that if you performed a morphing spell on someone, then you needed the potion to turn them back into themselves again. Something about reverse incantation, right? The potion was still seeping into the tiles. Could I get some of it back, just one tiny drop?

I set Allie down on the granite countertop and grabbed a random glass from inside the cupboard. I got on my hands and knees on the floor and tried to use my hands to scoop up the potion and get it back into the glass. For rather obvious reasons this wasn't going to work.

Panic flooded through me as I realized that I didn't have much time. Just as I reached for a plastic bottle cap, bluish smoke filled the room. Then all at once, when the smoke cleared, the only thing left of the potion was a bluish stain on the tiles. I cautiously touched the stain, but my hand came up totally dry.

Suddenly, I heard the unmistakable sound of Mom's car door slamming. I picked a scared-looking Allie up and raced upstairs to my room. After carefully setting her on my bed, I flew back downstairs to greet Mom.

She set down her Haute Couture shopping bag and smiled at me, pushing a lock of wavy, green-and-purple hair behind my ear.

"Hi, Zoey. Sorry I'm so late. The traffic was bad, and I got held up."

I glanced over at the clock. I hadn't even realized Mom was late. I started talking as fast as I could to distract her from realizing that Allie wasn't there. I figured that would buy me enough time to think about what to tell Mom.

"Oh, hi, Mom! It's fine that you're late; I sort of didn't notice that! Oh my gosh, I'm so excited about Krystal and Karen and maybe even Kiera coming over, aren't you? And can I invite some friends over to the movie theater on Sunday? And what's for dinner? Are you gonna make it the witchy way? Of course I like it better when you don't 'cause I like the anticipation, but it's so late so maybe you should, and also I think it might be cool if we ordered takeout or pizza—"

"Honestly, Zoey, you know there's no way whatsoever I am going to order takeout on a weekday. As it is your father has gone to the gym and is going to be very late coming home today. And where's your sister? She should be here for dinner. Where *is* she?"

This was the question I had been dreading. I rapidly changed the subject, not bothering to answer Mom's incessant queries. I didn't care much for takeout or pizza anyway.

"But *Mom*," I whined. "It's Friday, you know it is. On second thought, I don't really care. Maybe we should…"

"Honey, we are NOT ordering takeout today, is that clear? And where IS your sister? She should be on time for dinner."

"Syra's mom called to ask if Allie could come to her sleepover today, don't you remember? She came here to pick Allie up to go to her house at around six o'clock this afternoon. Allie should be home sometime tomorrow at around noon. So I guess we'll be having dinner together tonight." I was shocked at myself for the huge, whopper-sized lie I had just told.

"Hmm. I don't seem to remember her calling, do you?" Mom asked, clearly suspicious.

"I don't know. But you must have said yes because she left," I replied shakily. I felt miserable. Mom and Dad would find out about this eventually if I didn't undo the spell first. I would be dead!

After about half an hour, Dad came home. I had to lie to *him* this time and tell him about where Allie had supposedly gone. Apparently Allie was going to be back tomorrow just before lunch.

That night as I lay in bed cuddling Allie, I felt extremely restless (I mean, given the current circumstances, who wouldn't?), but it wasn't just concerning my little sister's fate. There was the bunny care. I'd never really been that obsessed with bunnies before and had no idea whatsoever of how to take care of them. Besides, as if the situation wasn't bad enough, I REALLY needed to get Allie back into a human before Mom and Dad found out what I'd done to her.

You know, it was terribly surprising how silent Allie was. You'd think she'd be hooting and hollering (or actually make that *purring,* since I did some research and bunnies actually *purr*) all over the place now that she was a bunny, and a very cute one at that. But it was obvious that she knew she shouldn't make a sound. Allie is aggravatingly idiotic when it comes to everyday things like cleaning her room without using magic, but when it comes to stuff like this she's not nearly that hopeless.

After a while I couldn't stay still anymore. I tiptoed silently to the upstairs railing, leaving Allie curled up peacefully on my bed. I tilted my head and listened for any evidence of stuff going on down there. I heard the clank of ceramic dishes against the side of the sink. The faucet was turned on and off. Clearly this would go on for a while. I might as well get some sleep.

I walked back to my bedroom before I heard a door close—or make that *slam*—in a not-so-quiet manner downstairs. I curiously made my way down, being careful to keep close to the railing.

I let myself into the kitchen. There was nobody there. I heard the sounds of teeth being brushed, so I headed to my parents' room. I crouched near the doorway and listened. It appeared that Mom and Dad were arguing about something.

I felt guilty, eavesdropping like this, with no real purpose. But all the same I listened, and I could easily hear all that was being said. My heart stood still as I realized what they were saying.

"David, I'm *sure* I didn't call Syra's mother to come pick Allie up for a sleepover. I checked the recents, and she wasn't on my list!"

"Caroline, you need to stay calm. You probably absent-mindedly deleted her name from the recents on your iPhone."

Strange how my parents always use each other's names when they're arguing.

"Seriously, David!" I imagined Mom throwing up her hands in exasperation. "I am sixty-five percent, that is sixty-five point *nine* percent sure she did not call. And even if she did, Allie should not have gone without at least calling *me* to say she was going. Especially with Zoey around to check!"

"Well, why don't you call Catherine back just to make sure?"

"David, it would seem so strange! I don't want her to think I was too occupied when talking to her on the phone to realize what she was saying. I don't want her to think I'm some sort of absent-minded doofus!"

I didn't need to listen anymore. I felt sick to my stomach. Sighing, I trooped back upstairs and shot into Dad's study, where he keeps his laptop and computer. I logged on, feeling like a crazy criminal, and began to do an extensive search on the products you can feed bunnies. I figured I could probably smuggle down some rabbit food tonight and give it to Allie. I knew I could feed her salad or carrots, but Mom might not have those things currently.

After reading down a Discovery Channel web page, I decided lettuce and parsley would do for now. After making sure my parental personnel had retired, I darted into the kitchen and raided the refrigerator. Allie had never liked lettuce before. (What do you expect? Kids never like vegetables!) But since she was currently a bunny, they'd have to work. Or else she would starve. And I couldn't allow that.

I got a bowl out from a cupboard (thankfully not the magic one) and ran upstairs. Allie could eat her meal when she woke up tomorrow morning. If she wanted to eat it, that was.

Five

I Get in a Close Scrape

I hardly got any sleep that night, and I awoke with bloodshot, reddish eyes. This was no surprise, considering I had gone to bed last night at around three o'clock. That might not seem so bad to you, as you might remember that it was a Saturday and I'd probably get to sleep in. But not that day.

The muffled ring of my alarm clock startled me and I sat up straight with a jolt. I took it out from under my fluffy, purple pillow and opened my light pink curtains to let the sunlight in—before I realized that there was no sunlight, as it was before 6:00 a.m....on a Saturday!

Allie dozed on and off even though the light was still on. I dug through my spell book collection and pulled one out that I thought might help.

The Power of Transformation, the title read. I opened it and turned to the chapter about undoing morphing spells. Everything there showed that you needed the original potion to reverse the enchantment, which ultimately meant death and doom for both myself as well as my little sister.

For two hours I leafed through about a dozen spell books, feeling hopelessly in despair. The whole series of books droned ridiculously bewilderingly, incomprehensibly, discombobulatingly, perplexingly, bafflingly, and incredibly mystifyingly unclear text. As in:

"......supplementary characteristics with various hexes and incantations adhered specifically to each metamorphose creation; necessary to morph them back into their original articulation and configuration......"

How could any witchery handbook be so incredibly boring and useless, especially when I was in such dire need of something even vaguely resembling help?!

I had to start thinking straight. If I didn't tell Mom and Dad, Allie might never be a human again. We would be devastated, and I could not, should not, *would* not allow that to happen. On the other hand, if I *did* tell, Mom would skin me alive—but still, they would call over a specialist to come help Allie. And she would be transformed. Back into a girl again. Hopefully...not that I love her that much. Actually, on second thought, I think I do.

I glanced back at my alarm clock and noticed how late it was—nearing seven thirty. Mom and Dad were early birds and would be up any moment. Where could I hide the bunny version of Allie until the time bomb exploded at exactly noon today?

The bottom of my bookcase seemed to be a most ridiculous but very suitable place. I flung out the books and bottom board-shelf and then stuffed a couple of polar fleece flannel sheets in for comfort. Regrettably I pushed Allie into the bookcase, assuring her that the bookcase had an adequately low center of gravity, and closed her in quietly. Allie did not, rather shockingly, make any attempt to escape. I could tell that she understood perfectly what was going on.

I heard the sounds of teeth being brushed and coffee being made downstairs. I slipped down. Dad looked up from over his papers.

"Hi, Zoey. I'll be going over to Jiffy for an oil change today. The old Chevy's gotten pretty cranky lately. You wanna come along?" he asked, sipping his coffee.

"Um, I think not...I have, like, a ton of homework this weekend. It's for a—a special project. In social studies," I bluffed, red in the face.

"That's OK, Zoey," Dad replied. "If Allie returns on time, we'll go to the mall this afternoon. We need to get you some new clothes. You've outgrown half your jeans already."

Oh, yeah. *That.* Normally I would be overjoyed at the idea of shopping for clothes and possibly some lip gloss, nail polish, and hair accessories, but not today. Just the thought of shopping on such a traumatizing day made me want to vomit with guilt.

After a rather silent breakfast, I met Mom in the hall. I told her I needed to work on my supposed social studies project about the greatest inventors in history, so she shouldn't disturb me. Mom looked disbelieving for a moment but then said OK, I could go. Just for cover I printed out a Wikipedia page or two about Benjamin Franklin and laid them out on my bed so that it would look like I was doing research.

I made sure the coast was clear and Mom and Dad were nowhere in sight. I let Allie out of the bookcase where I had hidden her. She curled up beside me on my bed. I almost laughed out loud at the thought of what Mom would do if she found out that a *bunny* was sleeping on my bed. Ha-ha. Very funny. But I had to focus on the task at hand.

I tried to think clearly. Evidently I needed a better plan than just leafing through witchy university-level textbooks, because that wouldn't get me anywhere if I wanted to reverse Allie's enchantment by noon. But...*what about the secret cupboard?* It was so obvious! I wondered why I hadn't thought of it before.

I remembered what had happened when I had wished for the bunny potion. It had taken me by surprise as it just appeared there magically, inside the cupboard. If I wished for a bunny rabbit enchantment *undoing* spell, what would I get?

I would have to be careful while doing this. One of my spells had already gone horribly wrong, and I couldn't afford to risk another one...or could I? I ran my mind over the numerous possibilities of what could happen to poor Allie if I messed with the magic cupboard again. Lots of things could happen, the worst of which I didn't want to admit to myself, let alone my sister. And perhaps most atrocious of all, I didn't even know the origin of the hidden storage space, or where it had come from. For all I knew, some crackbrained evil wizard had put it there to enchant our house and trick someone into thinking it would make all their dreams come true, when really it was a secret booby trap or something. OK, maybe I'm getting a little overboard with the whole evil wizard thing, but I guess you know what I'm talking about.

Hoping Mom wasn't in the kitchen, I carefully and quietly made my way downstairs. I peeked into the room nervously, ready to duck out of the way if someone saw me.

Too late.

Mom was in there, spreading peanut butter on whole-wheat bread for our lunch (she's really strict about that whole health-and-fitness pyramid thing). She looked up cheerily when she saw me.

"Hey, Zoey. When will you be ready for lunch? I might have to make something extra, because I just noticed that there is way less lettuce in the fridge than there should have been. Do you know anything about it?"

It took me a couple of moments to soak in what she'd just said.

The lettuce I fed Allie last night was supposed to be for lunch today.

I'll repeat that in case you didn't get it. THE LETTUCE I FED ALLIE LAST NIGHT WAS SUPPOSED TO BE FOR LUNCH TODAY!

✳ ✳ ✳

I gasped. I panicked. Now Mom and Dad would find out about what I had done to Allie, and they would be so so so so so so mad at me, and they would kick me out of the house. They would turn me over to the police. I would be named a JUVENILE DELINQUENT for good and forever! I would…I would…

Mom must have noticed my rumpled, more-than-slightly-disturbed state because she frowned and inquired, "Do you feel all right? What's wrong?"

I plastered a huge, fake grin on my face and said, feigning carefreeness (if that's even a word), "Huh? Oh, I'm fine. It's just…um…just nothing, you know?"

"No really, what's wrong?" Mom can be very determined when she wants to be.

"Seriously, it's nothing. I promise," I mumbled.

"All right then. Let's get on with this," Mom said, getting cheerful again. "So *will* I have to make something extra, or will I not?"

"I don't know," I answered, not trusting myself to say anything more.

"Zoey, did you take some lettuce yesterday?" Mom pressed. There was no getting out of this now.

It might actually have been funny if I'd said, "*Oh yes, I'm quite sure I DID take the lettuce and some of the parsley last night, but it was only to feed my little sister, whom you may happen to know I turned into a cute little bunny without your permission and can't seem to change back again,*" but of course I was too smart to do that. So I just had to stand there miserably, gripping the granite countertop with my nails and chipping my French manicure as I thought of what to say.

Mom gave me a strange look. "It's OK if you got hungry last night and took them," she said, although her voice told me that she didn't exactly mean it. "I guess I'll have to make something new for now, so just remember to tell me next time."

I regained my senses and smiled at Mom. "Yeah, I guess I *did* kind of get hungry yesterday," I admitted sheepishly.

Still looking highly suspicious (there was a reason for that; why in the entire witchy universe would I touch my veggies?!), Mom said, "Hmm. OK. But please remember to ask me next time, all right?"

I nodded and hightailed it out of that kitchen in a hurry.

I went upstairs and locked myself in my room. I needed to think things out right then. If I couldn't get into the kitchen to use the magic compartment, then my attempts to cure Allie would prove to be a series of epic fails, and Mom and Dad would find out about them. But when could I use the cupboard? I glanced over at the clock like I'd been doing only about a million and a half times so far. 9:06 a.m.?! Only an *hour* had passed since I saw Dad in the dining room! It had seemed like *eight* hours. I was beginning to feel like one of those princesses in silly fairy tales who have to break the enchantment by midnight or else their husbands will be turned into evil wizards. Except in this case it was my *sister* whose health and well-being was in jeopardy, and not my husband's. Fortunately. I think.

I considered. If I could find a way to get Mom out of the kitchen, I could get to the cupboard and reverse the morphing spell. That wouldn't be too hard. Maybe if I told her I wanted to make some cooking project as a surprise she would get out of there. But she was preparing lunch or something, wasn't she?

I had a lot of time. I could study algebra for my big test coming up next week. As you can probably tell by now, algebra isn't one of my best areas, and I was just barely keeping up a B- in that particular subject. I was going to have to study, or else Ms. Davidson would really have something to get me for then. Yep, that was something I'd do. I marched upstairs confidently before I heard Mom's voice floating up. Again! OMG! Wait, and she told me she was in CHOIR when she was a kid? No way!

Mom sounded mad. Like, really mad. Fiery mad.

"Zara Sapphire Williams, GET DOWN HERE THIS MINUTE!"

Darn it! I was really going to get it now. I racked my brain to think of what I could have done wrong over the last few days, but I couldn't think of anything. Except for maybe turning Allie into a bunny, which just so happens to be the worst possible thing I have done in my entire miserable life so far.

I rushed downstairs and what I saw did not even vaguely resemble a disaster requiring emphasized anger or disappointment. Mom was examining the bluish stain the potion left when it soaked into the tiles. She looked up and realized that I was there.

"Zoey, why are the tiles such a bright blue here? What have you been doing?"

OK, that was unfair for two hugely gigantic reasons. One, the tiles were NOT *bright* blue, and two, how did she know *I* had caused the vandalism? Even if I had.

"Um," I said apprehensively. "I must have spilled something. Like food coloring. Or something."

"Zoey, don't you know that you aren't allowed to play with items in here without permission from either me or your father?"

I sighed. This WAS my fault. It WAS *so* my fault. Like, TOTALLY my fault. I was the one who had turned Allie into a bunny in the first place using that blue potion, and I was probably the one who was going to get punished for it. So I knew I had at least better own up to having turned the bright white tiles in the kitchen pale blue and get this whole annoying thing over with.

"Yeah, I do know I'm not supposed to play with stuff in here, and I guess I did do it, and I'm sorry about it," I admitted quietly, hoping that saying sorry would help me get out of trouble.

"With what?" Mom does not let things like this slip that easily. She folded her arms across her chest and looked at me with an expectant expression.

Thinking quickly, I said, "Oh, probably some food coloring I was experimenting with. You know, to make those tissue-paper rocks I told you about."

Tissue-paper rocks? That was so totally random! But Mom must not have thought so, because she let me off the hook. Almost.

"Well, don't do it again. And I want you to have this cleaned up within ten minutes' time. And not using magic. *Now!*"

Score! Mom walked out of the kitchen, leaving me to go on with my work by myself. I snapped my fingers twice, muttered an incantation, and made the blue stain simultaneously disappear. Much as I hated disobeying Mom, it had to be done this time.

I tore to the other side of our gigantic kitchen and moved away the coffee maker from where the compartment should be.

I took one glance at the teapot-shaped handle and remembered how to open it. *Outward and upward. Carefully.*

To my intense shock, the thing didn't budge! I pushed. I pulled. I tugged upward and outward and downward. I tried various combinations of the three. Nothing worked. I even knocked on the smooth, deep cherry wood to make sure that there was something beyond it. It didn't sound hollow like I had expected it to sound. Instead, the sound came out thick, as if I were knocking on solid rock.

I snapped back to the horrendous, nightmarish present as I heard Mom's highly impatient voice.

"Zoey, are you done in there?! It's past nine thirty! I REALLY need to make lunch! Remember that I wanted to make that new recipe, and that will take time! Allie will be here any moment, and I want her to be here for the new delicacy!"

What new delicacy?

Then, upon hearing Allie's name, my stomach twisted itself into a terribly complex Indonesian knot (actually I don't know whether Indonesian knots exist or not, but a girl has to have some imagination, doesn't she?). It was truly a miracle that it didn't snap in two and break itself.

But if you think about it, what did my mom need so much time for? To create an intellectual, creative dish, as in a cooking show?

Yeah, right.

Because really, she's not going to be on the Food Network anytime soon.

But I had to figure out the mystery of the teapot handle, because it wasn't opening. I gave myself a short pep talk to calm my nerves. *You can do this, Zoey. You have the intellectual ability. You have the wits, the guts, the brains, Zoey! You have the—*

Unfortunately, Mom cut short my cute little façade of determination with her highly consistent yelling. Really, it's amazing that she doesn't get bronchitis.

"Zoey! What did I tell you? Is the stain permanent, or have I not made myself clear?"

OK, this was it. Either I fixed this issue right now, as in *this instant,* or else I was doomed. Maybe not technically doomed, but my sister might be.

I chanted an opening spell under my breath. Nothing happened. Willing with everything I had, I tried again. Still nothing.

The kitchen door abruptly and most unceremoniously burst open. Mom looked in with a superfluously aggravated expression on her face. She looked down at the floor. I gulped. The entire stain was gone without a trace, so I had no idea what I was so worried about. Well, with the exception of...oh, you know.

"It's all gone?" Mom inspected the tiled floor closely, clearly suspicious for a reason that I could not identify.

"Yep," I answered with as much confidence as I could possibly muster under the horribly rotten circumstances.

"Good. Now go up to your room and work on your *project* while I cook lunch." The unnecessary emphasis on the word *project* only amplified my belief that Mom had qualms about whether or not I was working on a social studies report.

As I dejectedly trudged upstairs, my flustered mind ran over all of the things my parents could do to me if, no, *when,* they found out about my predicament. Most of the possibilities would probably violate at least a *few* of my basic Constitutional rights.......

The amendment states......	What could my parents do to me that violates it?
1. Freedom of speech, religion, petition the government for a redress of grievances, etc.	Let's not even get into this one. What kind of kid even HAS freedom of speech anyway?!
2. Right to a well-regulated militia, right to bear arms......	I most certainly may not have weapons, and it's too cold in December for strapless dresses, don't you think?
3. No soldier shall be quartered in a homeowner's house without prior consent......	If my room was strictly my territory and my parents were the soldiers, they could easily invade.
4. The right of the people to be secure in their persons, houses, and effects......	My belongings are ALWAYS being searched without reason!
5. No person shall be held to answer for a crime for a capital, unless in the presence of a jury......	I don't know about you, but *my* parents aren't going to hire a jury any time soon! I guess I could conjure one up using my magical powers, but my parents would zap it right back home to where it belonged. Dream on, Zoey!

6. The accused shall enjoy the right to a speedy and...get this...PUBLIC trial?!	I have to say about this one, I don't exactly want my trial to be public, especially as witchcraft is strictly kept secret within the witch society...
7. No one accused of a crime shall be tried for the same crime twice in a court of law.	Pretty basic, if you ask me. Yet that happens often. Arguments between my mom and I can go on for days on end.
8. Prevention of cruel or unusual punishments, excessive bails, etc.	Are you kidding me?! My parents OFTEN inflict illogical, cruel and unusual punishments on me, such as taking away my cell phone or making me study algebra in a time warp, with zero breaks, for a few days!
9. Peoples' rights are not limited to those in the Constitution......	Oh, all right, nobody actually violates THAT aspect of the Constitution. Or at least I *hope* so!
10. Oh yeah, and the powers not granted to the federal government shall be granted to the states or individuals...	I never get to decide my own rights. But then again, who does?

See what I mean? There are dozens of ways you can be punished if you're a regular girl, but being a witchy human just takes the cake (or lemon-scented potion) in the punishments category.

I'd never been so despondent in my whole life.

Six

One Scary Visitor

No! I sat straight up and gasped. This couldn't be happening. It just couldn't. How was this my life?!

It was all a strange and unpleasant dream, I told myself. I had not just fallen asleep over my spell technique books while my sister had a nearly irreversible enchantment locked over her. It was not 11:56 a.m. And my parents were not sitting cool as ice downstairs, not ever imagining that this was not a wonderful, normal day, but potentially the worst, most terrible day of a person's whole entire life. None of this was happening to me right now…because I was a good witch, and horrid things hardly ever happen to good witches. Not while they're practicing spell technique and being good little girls, at least.

But I was a rare case. I was doomed!

Completely, utterly, starkly, downright, DOOMED!

Rich vocabulary, huh? I took a moment to think about that as I sat on my bed and watched the clock. It was a welcome distraction. Any moment now Mom would be calling Julia's parents and demanding to know why her daughter was so late home from a slumber party.

In actuality, of course, my mother was calmly dishing out handfuls of cranberries over miniature piles of sour cream salad and hoping her family would enjoy her newfound talent—creating colorful salads. If salads were a genre, my mom would have all of the library's books that belonged to that genre checked out under her name.

However, my current situation was neither as calm nor as serene as the remainder of my family's was. Allie curled up at my feet and whimpered pitifully. I lifted her into my lap. By the expression on her fuzzy little face I could tell she was attempting to explain something. Or maybe she wanted to make inquiries as to whether or not she would ever be a *Homo sapien* again. Taking a deep breath, I sat there and expounded on and on about what had happened. And I told her how absolutely SORRY I was about this, and about how nothing like this could ever happen to her again. I talked faster than I had ever talked before, but by the end of it, the innocent-looking Princess Vera Wang alarm clock on my bedside table showed 11:59 a.m.

Never had I hated an electronic device so much in my entire life. If only I could turn back the clock, just another couple of hours or so, I could figure out what to do. I could fix this overpowering dilemma. I could…I could…

Anyway, this pep talk/lecture went on for a little while. It really wasn't like me to lecture myself like this, but now I understood what Mom meant when she talked about *decisions you will regret for the rest of your life.* Oh all right, maybe not technically the rest of my life, but long enough to figure out that I had learned a lesson.

By now, of course, it was past noon. Dad had come back from Jiffy, and I could hear his off-tuned singing all the way up in my room. I covered my ears and plugged in my MP3 player. Allie bumped her head against my legs, and I could tell that she wanted to do the same. Any other time it would have made me laugh. But not today.

I could hear Mom telling him to be quiet. "Your singing makes my eardrums hurt," she complained. "Why you couldn't just stay at the Jiffy and leave me alone to continue my day in peace, I simply cannot imagine. Why, how *you* manage to tolerate your *own* voice is beyond me!"

Over the blasting One Direction and Mariah Carey songs coming from my MP3 player, I could still hear my parents. "No, lunch is most definitely not ready yet," Mom was saying. "I am trying out a new cheesy lasagna and salad recipe; can't you see that I'm working on it? Please let me work in tranquility whilst you find yourself something productive to do away from the kitchen. Actually, on second thought, now why don't you make yourself useful and load the dishwasher for me? Oh, no, NONE of the dishes are ready yet! When Catherine comes over to drop Allie off, I want to have her stay for lunch. It's basic hospitality! Yikes, the dishes will NEVER be ready! See, it's already way, *way* past twelve!"

Liar! It's not even noon yet!

"Not everyone's as late as we always are, you know! So load the dishwasher whilst I get on with my cooking!" Mom always seems to use weird English words like *whilst* when she's annoyed, upset, or, more precisely, angry. In this case, at least.

As far as I could tell, Dad had been standing there patiently listening to Mom's ranting about our family habits. *Eyeroll.* I would have flown off the handle hours ago.

Then it hit me: Any moment now, the time bomb would go off. If Mom was really expecting Catherine—that would be Syra's mom—to stay here for lunch, that would only feed her inconceivable fury when she realized that Allie had been enchanted. By none other than her own daughter!

I heard Mom's voice floating up the stairs again, breaking my concentration on the Princess Vera Wang alarm clock. "Catherine will be here any minute. Are you finished with the dishes? Good. The meal is almost done. Just another squirt...there. It looks so pretty!" I could just visualize her stepping back to admire her handiwork.

"Yes. Very nice," Dad agreed admiringly. "I'm so hungry! I can't wait to taste that cheesy lasagna." *He must be checking his watch,* I thought. *Time is ticking down rapidly.* "And," Dad added, "that salad looks bee-yoo-ti-ful!"

"Well, your hunger impulses will just have to wait," Mom snapped, her irritation flaring up again as it does nearly 24/7. Except this time, it must have been because of Dad's singing beginning again.

I simply had to wonder why Mom wasn't panicking. After all, it *was* a quarter past twelve. Maybe she suspected something? But why? Besides her suspicions about my supposed social studies project, she had no reason to imagine I had anything to do with Allie's possible nonappearance. Still, did I tell you that for some reason my parents have a knack for psychic abilities? Not that I really believe in psychic abilities, unless of course you cast a time lapse/hypnotic spell on someone. Attempting that is a very dangerous undertaking. Only expert witches and wizards generally try it.

My mind was drawn back to the clock after a moment. Suddenly I saw a frail, old-looking, but kind witch's face staring back at me, with wispy grayish hair and deep wrinkles. It had to be my imagination, right? I mean, the face was kind of drifting over the clock. I tried to shake the image, but for some reason it didn't budge. I gasped in amazement and terror as I realized that the face wasn't just something I was imagining. It was *real.*

Seven

My Secret Is Discovered

This surreal *face* was smiling at me and appeared to be making a supreme effort to speak. While one might think that this bizarre creature was a *ghost,* it most indubitably was not. Witches and wizards do not believe in *ghosts.* Why, just the thought of *ghosts* is known to cause some witches to contract a fever of 103 degrees or more.

So if this apparition-like thing was not a *ghost,* then logical reasoning led me to think it was another witch. Gaining back my senses, I watched it closely and realized that I was not frightened. Such a nice, affectionate face could not belong to an enemy. But this face did not have a body, which meant that it was not the witch herself, but rather a duplicate of the original being. The actual witch was somewhere far away, perhaps in a remote corner of the universe, which the mistiness of the figure led me to believe.

The duplicate being's feeble voice, etched with worry, wrenched me from my deep daydream. "Zoey," it said. I shivered. How did it know my name?

"Zoey," it repeated. The air became purplish and got a sort of shimmery quality to it. The witch's full body materialized in a shower of glittering diamonds, which lay scattered on the floor beside my beautiful aqua rug.

"I am the head of the witchy society. I don't think we have met before."

"No, we haven't," I answered carefully.

Suddenly there was a whooshing noise. The head of the witchy community or whoever she was disappeared, simultaneously dousing me in silver sparkles. I heard footsteps coming up. Panicking, I stuffed a freaked-out Allie into my bookcase and shut the door, not bothering to put in a few blankets for comfort, as I was breathing hard and almost hyperventilating with anticipation.

Almost instantly Mom came into the room. She sat down on the edge of my bed. My heart just about stopped beating as I realized that I had nothing to prove I had been working on this the whole time. I groaned as I imagined the punishments she could inflict on me. For example, taking away my makeup was a horrendously bad one. It is a cruel and unusual punishment. Come to think of it, I probably would've had to take legal action if things came to that.

"So, Zoey," Mom murmured kind of—dare I say it?—dreamily. Then her voice hardened. "We need to talk. Can you explain to me what happened to Allie yesterday while your father and I were gone?"

Time seemed to stand still for the few seconds in between Mom's queries and my answer. My mind raced as I thought of a hundred measly, really lame excuses.

Um. I went to do my homework and she just...uh... you know, disappeared? Into midair. Wait, actually, an evil wizard came over and enchanted her. Now she's a spider living in the attic. I was sort of helpless in the situation, you know?

But my gut feeling was that I had to tell the truth. So tell the truth I did. Or at least I *prepared* to tell the truth. Instead, Allie had to go and reveal herself like the naughty, headstrong but very cute little spitfire she really is.

A soft purr. Scratch, scratch.

I stood paralyzed in shock.

"Zoey? Did you just—"

"No," I replied quickly, too quickly. Immediately Mom became on alert.

Scratch. Purr. Soft whimper.

Now Mom was REALLY perplexed. "Zoey!" she reprimanded sternly. "Really! What have you been doing with the—"

What she would say next I was rather glad I did not know. Of course, my not knowing it was not much of a help, because of course Allie had to go and unveil her enchanted identity further.

WHAM! And then, *"Squeeeeeeeeeeeeeeeee!"*

Mom leaned against the wall and gasped, as if to catch her breath after a traumatizing incident.

"Zoey," she whispered faintly, "is there an *animal* in this room?!"

Eight

Strangely Calm

I avoided looking into Mom's eyes. What was she going to do? Cry? Say how disappointed she was? Yell at me? Lecture me? She hadn't said anything for the last few seconds, and I was *just dying* to know which, or actually *how many*, of the following I was:

1. A bad influence on my sister,
2. The worst, most irresponsible daughter in the world,
3. A very foolish, ridiculous girl who was about to get grounded…permanently!
4. Most disobedient and terribly deceitful,
5. Extremely disappointing to my parents,
6. Or maybe…Oh well, I'm pretty tired of listing the possibilities anyway.

You know how you feel when your parents are reading over your gigantic pile of math homework and don't say anything about it, and the desire to know what they think is just about killing you? Well, that's how I felt then. Except about a million times worse.

No, make that sixteen hundred eighty-eight million, seventeen thousand sixty-four. Give or take a few.

So when Mom actually *smiled,* and looked perfectly happy, you can imagine how freaked out I felt.

"Um, Mom?!" I cried, flustered. "Why the heck are you smiling?"

"I get it. One of your ridiculous 'magic' tricks again," Mom grinned. "But change her back right now, because it's almost time for lunch and she'll be hungry."

"Mom!" I gasped. Did she really think that I was playing around?!

"But really..." Mom's voice trailed off.

"No, Mom! Oh, I am SO sorry. You don't know HOW sorry I am! I turned Allie into a bunny rabbit with the magic cupboard in the kitchen, without your permission! And now I can't change her back again! I know this is my fault! I shouldn't have done it! And you should know, I, like, totally get that! But the potion seeped into the tiles, and that was the blue stain you saw in the kitchen, and I lied about that too! And since you need the potion to turn the bunny back into Allie again, she might stay enchanted forever! Please help me! I am, like, UNIMAGINABLY sorry about that! Oh my God! I am, like, so totally the absolute WORST daughter ever! Punish me! Ground me! Torture me! Sell me to the butcher as a slave [extremely random]! Do whatever you want to me! But please, PLEASE bring my sister back! And—"

"Oh please, Zoey," Mom moaned, touching her hand to her forehead in mock exasperation. "You can give me such a headache sometimes. This is NOT the time!"

"But Mom," I gasped in utter disbelief.

"Hey Zoey," Mom said suddenly, staring around at my room and looking bewildered, "*what* project did you say you were working on? You don't seem to have gotten anything done so far!"

OK, so maybe Mom had found out about this issue and I had to tell her the truth, but since it had happened and I couldn't reverse the events (well, technically I could using magic, but I didn't know how to), I decided it was best to confess to all of my dreadfully farfetched mistakes at once. Honesty, you know? Like what all those nerds are obsessed with. And trustworthiness.

"A social studies project." I sighed. *Not!*

"And...you have no work to show for it?" Mom wasn't giving me a chance to collect my thoughts properly! But then again, I probably didn't deserve one.

"That was a lie. I already told you, but you didn't listen. You thought I was just playing. But I wasn't! I turned Allie into a bunny using that potion I found in the cupboard, and I can't change her back again! I need your help! Seriously! I don't want a bunny for a sister!"

"You...t-turned...your little sister into a *b-b-b-unny*?!"

Mom really looked as if she were on the verge of fainting. I earnestly considered steadying her, but I figured it didn't suit the situation all that well.

Then she recovered herself and looked relieved. "I knew that you were behind in your witchiness studies and reverse incantation techniques, but I had no idea it was *that* bad! Bring me the potion and we'll fix this," she instructed authoritatively.

My face paled. "You still don't get it," I muttered. "I don't have the potion anymore."

"You *don't?*"

"No. That was the blue stain in the kitchen, remember?"

Another gasp for air. "Oh, no! We will have to call over an expert!"

She reached for the doorknob, looking pensive. I ran after her. "Mom, I'm sorry! I had no idea that this would happen to us."

To my relief, Mom was only mildly angry. "I know that. You were annoyed with her and wanted her off your hands for a while, that's all—and I can see that it turned into quite a disaster. Can I see her for a minute? Where is she?"

Sheepishly I opened my bookcase. Mom stared at it in amazement and said a silent prayer to the sky. "What a ridiculous hiding place! I honestly *can't* imagine what this household is coming to!"

She lifted Allie out of it and hugged her. I still don't get how she could love that ludicrous little mischief-maker so much.

"But it worked," I said.

"It sure did. You had me fooled for a while, all right." Then she actually laughed.

Mom walked out with Allie in her arms. What an absurd situation! It was pure irony! First I turn my little sister into a bunny rabbit without permission and tell a whole bunch of lies. Then Mom finds out and thinks it's a trick. And when I actually tell her that it's not one, she thinks it's so hilarious! Adults! *Eyeroll.*

My mom was right. This household really is unbelievable. Unbelievably crazy, that is!

Nine

Out of Control

Lunch was a very mild and restrained affair compared to what I'd thought it would be. No shouting, crying, screaming, yelling, scolding, lecturing, preaching, wailing, hollering, bellowing, bawling, howling, shrieking, screeching, or otherwise horribly puerile disciplinary tactics were carried out. Thankfully I hadn't had to listen to Mom inform Dad of the dreadful reality. She'd taken care of the little revelation where I couldn't hear her talk. When my parents are discussing me, I have this sinking feeling that it's better to keep my distance.

That's not to say that I didn't get into trouble. If you ask me, the worst trouble was the guilt I felt after committing this sort of crime. If my parents had decided to administer a harsh punishment, I think I probably would not have minded. It was better than the silence I was feeling now, anyway. I could tell Mom and Dad were disappointed in me, and seeing that fuzzy little bunny actually *sitting* at the *dining table* only made me feel worse. Believe me, if Allie were a real bunny and not really my younger sister, then she most definitely wouldn't be happily positioned in that sort of location. (Look out, ceramic plates! I think you've just met your first real rival! Meet my pet bunny and so-called little sister, Allie!)

After lunch, Mom and Dad and I had a very uncomfortable family meeting, like they do in books and reality shows. Actually, we had never had a family meeting before, so I was more than a little worried. We all sat at the dining table as if at a round-table conference (and the dining table in my house really is round), with notepads in front of us and Allie cuddled down in my lap. I stared at her and pretended to be absolutely mesmerized by her fluffy tail and cuteness. Amazingly, I didn't even look up once for the possible two to three minutes we sat there without saying a word to each other, so I guess my intense staring was rather conspicuous after all. *Nice way to get out of an unpleasant chitchat, Zoey!*

"So," Mom said after a moment or two (or actually, make that **666** moments: I counted), "it looks like we have a little dilemma on our hands. Zoey, do you have anything to say about this?"

I gulped nervously. What Mom had just said sounded very much like the beginning of a person's trial for execution purposes. And, most unfortunately, Mom was the jury. So I resolved to just sit quietly and not say anything. I stared at Mom, and she stared back. This strenuous staring competition went on for a little while, so I figured it was better to say something to shatter the tension into infinitesimal pieces.

"I guess you know all about what happened," I murmured quietly.

"Yes, but we want to hear *your* side of the story," Dad insisted.

So of course I had to go and tell him *exactly* what had happened, *exactly* how I did it, and, perhaps most importantly (to my parents, at least), *exactly* WHY I did it.

You don't need to know everything that was said, but you should know, I did get quite a lot written down on my notepad. And it wasn't just about witchcraft practice.

Dad, apparently, wanted to call over a specialist and get the whole rotten affair over with. But Mom had an entirely different idea, and I had to say I agreed with her more than with Dad. It was going to take more than an expert to fix this irrational, ridiculous situation. We were gonna have to call over the head of the witch society. With whom, at least as far as I knew, I'd had an extremely creepy encounter earlier. I told Mom about it and she agreed that this definitely needed figuring out.

Unfortunately, no one in my family knew the spell to call her over, and nobody's magic was strong enough to bring her back from wherever she was in the witchy universe. We'd just have to wait and see.

After sitting on my bed and thinking about this for a little while, I realized that my cousins, Karen, Kiera, and Krystal (my aunt has a thing for *K*s; it's one of the numerous mysteries of life, such as how socks "mysteriously" disappear in the dryer) were coming over this weekend. This may have been fun if it weren't for my sister's current state.

You see, my cousins are not witches. There must have been a genetic issue or something, because although my grandparents are all witches, none of my aunts and uncles are. So maybe none of my cousins captured the witchy genes. At least I'm here to carry on the tradition.

So as you can probably tell by now, this constituted a large problem. Karen is six years old, but Kiera is thirteen (my age), and Krystal is sixteen. Sixteen-year-olds ask questions! If Allie wasn't there, Krystal would want to know where she was, and why she wasn't with us. That put me into a major dilemma. As ironic as it seemed, I was really hoping that the chief of the witch community would come and rescue me from this...um...*predicament!*—oh yeah, that's the word. Or maybe not. I was still spooked by her sudden appearance. This was so NOT good. This was not good at all! I paced around my room in frustration, parting my swishy, sparkly curtains along the way, as if for inspiration. Allie hopped with me like she thought this was some sort of game. I had to admit, it was cute, but not much of a help to me. I kept on pacing, barely noticing where I was going, until I bumped into the wall. Hard. I left a deep indentation in the lavender-flowers-and-pink-swirls mural on my wall. One of the deep sea aqua leaf stickers I had magically conjured up and stuck on the wall fluttered to the ground. Oh well, I could fix that later. Rubbing my leg where I had bumped into the wall, I wandered aimlessly down the staircase. It was then, of course, that the head-of-society witch had to appear. I almost fell to the ground as I realized the creepy stuff that was happening. Hey, it's her own fault if I think she's creepy! She was the one who appeared to me without warning in the first place. I leaned against the wall, feeling sort of like I was about to faint, like Mom had done when she found out that I was hiding a *bunny* in my bookcase. I still roll my eyes at that, even though her facial expression *was* funny, I guess, when it had happened.

The appearance started as the usual delicate fluttering of diamonds to the ground. I don't exactly know why, but I picked them up and put them in my pocket as they came. Besides the fact that they were pretty, they were also a sort of keepsake for me. I think.

As she materialized in front of me, I got the strange feeling that I was being watched by someone other than myself. It might have been her presence, of course, but it made me jittery. And anyone could tell that I didn't like this old witch anyway. She should mind her own business in her own secret corner of the Milky Way galaxy instead of interfering with my life. My life was as complicated as it could possibly get without her highly unpleasant presence in it all the time.

Once she had fully materialized in front of me, I forced myself to smile. Getting on this witch's nerves did not seem like a good idea. Anyway, maybe she could help me. Maybe we could work this out together.

In her usual unsettling manner, she said my name. Again. I couldn't hear the clank of dishes or the tap being turned on and off downstairs. It was all very sinister. I wouldn't want to be alone with this spooky lady (hey, who'd blame me?)! But I had to say *something,* so I gripped the stair railing desperately and mumbled, "Hi."

"Why *hello*, Zoey!" she exclaimed as if I were the coolest thing that had ever happened to her. "I am so glad that you are at home. I simply don't know *what* I would have done with myself if I hadn't been available to help you. You see, you are in a bit of a quandary here. In fact, you have gotten yourself into a whole bundle of problems with your highly childish, infantile, immature, and highly insistent misuse of spells, potions, and incantations."

That sure sounded a whole lot like the opening to a United Nations assembly meeting. I bit my lips, but it didn't keep my cheeks from turning a shade of fuchsia that I didn't even know existed.

"Why, don't look so miserable at the mention of it! Of course, I am not *angry* with you, so I hope you don't think that," the witch continued aggravatingly. "Why, I myself suffered such casualties when I was your age..."

Casualties? That was definitely an exaggeration. Maybe even a hyperbole.

"So I looked through my crystal ball and deemed that helping you was, by far, the best choice..."

"Wait. Are we talking about psychic abilities from divination here, or about helping me with the issues that resulted from my '*highly childish, infantile, imma-ture, and highly insistent misuse of spells, potions, and incantations?*'" I snapped a little too viciously for the current circumstances, especially as this witch had no intention of locking me in the Alcatraz prison (or at least I hoped not).

"Oh, yes. I must remain on track," the witch said before adjusting her...*pigtails?!* Omigosh! Why was she wearing PIGTAILS?! Actually, I hadn't even noticed she had them until now! Come to think of it, she looked pretty funny with them sticking out of her gray hair-covered head.

I giggled. I couldn't help it. I guess the witch must have noticed it too, because she looked at me with an amused expression on her wrinkly face. "In a civi-lized community, old ladies wear pigtails and little girls straighten and style their hair at a hair salon—no, no, not a salon, it's actually called a *salad*—after using Pantene shampoo and conditioner," she explained passionately.

"Um…I-I guess that *sort of* makes sense," I stuttered helplessly. I mean, what could you do with a slightly—no, MAJORLY—mentally unhinged and eccentric witch like that?

"So back to the point, Zoey," she addressed me. To be honest, I was a little surprised she hadn't gotten off track like she did before. "We need to help you with step one—now that your cousins are coming tomorrow and staying here the entire long weekend, how are you going to distract them from Allison Mariah?"

"Um, if you'll excuse me from being rude, she likes to be called Allie. And I have a feeling that I'm smart enough to handle this situation myself," I shot back defensively. "And besides, first I at least need to know what to call you, don't I?"

"Now that you mention it. Zara, I would prefer for you not to call me *Mrs.* Anything."

I just stared at her.

"It makes me feel old, not at all like the highly attractive young woman I really am. But there are the downsides, of course. Just yesterday someone informed me that mistaking myself for a twenty-year-old girl doesn't count as me really being one. So, as I said, don't call me *Mrs.* anything. It makes me feel like an ancient old grandma."

"Feel?" I muttered viciously.

"Zara, please, be patient. For now, I would like for you to call me Cleopatra Hypnotica Hooshonicus."

"You want me to call you *what*?!" I said, my blood pressure skyrocketing.

"I *said*," she answered irritably, "that I would like to be called *Cleopatra Hypnotica Hooshonicus.* It is a simply beautiful name that signifies and pays a tribute to me, the pretty young queen of Egypt."

"You're not Cleopatra," I said accusingly. "You're the head of the witchy society...or so you claim."

"As I am. But you see, I really was Cleopatra when I was young. Unfortunately, they were really behind back then—no technology. I got bored. I was never killed by a serpent to avoid capture by the Romans; that's a myth. Instead, I time traveled. And I must have had the powers to hypnotize people with my immensely stunning gorgeousness."

"Whatever. I give up," I said, befuddled. "I'll just call you Cleo."

"Very honorable decision on your part, Zoey," she responded. "Now then, what were we talking about?"

"Something about my sister..."

"Oh yes, what are we to do when your cousins come over? If I could, I would have you handle this immense undertaking by yourself, as I have a terribly busy schedule lately; however, I cannot do that. You are too youthful and deprived of prior expertise in such an obfuscated field as witchcraft to handle the conundrum you're in. I shall have to help you. Now, on the point. Because of your current situation, you shall have to make Allison Mariah a clone of her original self. In other words, she will need a duplicate."

Now, *that* was something worth listening to. Overstimulated by this new and exciting information, I started to jump up and down (a terribly risky and hazardous move while standing precariously on the upper edge of a staircase). "Oh my gosh, that is, like, the coolest thing I've ever heard in the past thirty seconds!" I almost screeched. "I found a book with stuff on clones on my parents' bookshelf too! Oh, and can you make me a clone too? So I can skip school and witchy study sessions whenever I like, y'know?! And also I wanna learn how to time travel! OMG! This is the awesomest thing I've heard in the past forty-eight seconds! Wait, it couldn't have been that long while I was talking. On second thought, maybe I should keep track of the seconds that pass in order to get a better sense of time, you know?! And—"

"Let's cut down on the decibel level here. In fact, I think that our plans should not be discussed in front of your parents until further notice is given. By me, that is! Oh no, I think I have another call. It's an emergency! Yikes! As horribly impertinent, rude, obnoxious, selfish, self-centered, arrogant, insolent, impudent, disrespectful, impolite, brazen, brash, and cheeky it seems, I'm terribly sorry! I really *have* to go!"

She disappeared abruptly, leaving behind her usual shimmery diamond trail. I blushed the shade of an outrageously moldy, putrid apple. This witch was (or seemed to be) crazy and worrisome and had extremely farfetched ideas, but I couldn't help thinking that I had been every adjective she had just used when I spoke to her.

To distract myself, I began to wonder why she always left that diamond trail whenever she appeared or disappeared. Could I do the same? I had never universe traveled before. I guess it depended, eventually, on how magically sophisticated my skills were.

But of course, I had to concentrate on getting the potion for Allie. The problem was I had absolutely no idea of how to do it. Maybe if I made the potion again a miracle would happen (yeah right!) and I could change her back. Still, I guess it was worth a try.

So I made my way into the kitchen, which, thankfully, was vacant, and started to mix together the potion necessary to turn someone into a bunny, which I had memorized the day I enchanted Allie. I certainly wasn't messing with that evil cupboard again! Honestly, it acted as if it were a bad omen! Like, um, Satan, I think.

Unfortunately, I soon realized that the ground-up lettuce I needed had been fed to Allie. What would happen if I used, say, mint leaves as a substitute for lettuce? Maybe…just maybe…it would work. I felt relieved that I had memorized the ingredients for the potion that I had tried to make earlier, so now I knew them almost by heart. But *honestly,* changing out mint leaves for lettuce…

Potion making is, not surprisingly, one of the worst areas of witchcraft to mess around in.

In a few minutes, I had finished preparing the potion. Unfortunately, it didn't look like the pale blue potion that I had made before. Instead, it seemed to be…pinkish. I was suspicious; I wanted to make sure that it was the correct potion before doing anything with it. I let some of the mixture ooze over my fingers, and it felt cool, like what they put on your face at a body therapy salon.

Most unfortunately for me, that feeling didn't last very long.

A fiery sensation crept over my whole body. Had just *touching* the potion really activated it? Was this what it felt like to be turned into a bunny? If it was, I wasn't sure that I liked it very much. In fact, it was *horrible*! The fiery sensation was getting stronger.

The room began to spin around me. The sofas whirled around faster and faster, and I could just make out Dad laughing at me over his paperwork. Seems like he'd never witnessed anyone spinning around like a maniac before. I felt annoyed. What was I supposed to do anyway?

Ten

Time Traveling Just Isn't My Passion

Suddenly, I found myself being plummeted out of the room and into…was it—*outer space?* I didn't know what was happening or where I was going, but it didn't look all that interesting to me. More like swirling through space, staring at red-hot nebulae and galaxies. Generally, I guess I would've been a little more interested, but I was too freaked out to notice the splendor. I tried to recall something from one of my witchcraft textbooks, and then, miraculously, I remembered. This journey was exactly like what the authors had described in *Wizardry* Volume One—*TIME TRAVELING!*

Then, all at once, I felt as if I was spiraling through a black hole. If this was what time travel always felt like, I wasn't sure if I liked it.

Sure enough, when I landed, out of breath (FINALLY! Riding through space isn't as much fun as it sounds), I came through with a gentle touchdown. I looked around myself and saw miniature sapphires materializing around me.

Unfortunately, I was far too worked up to notice; I could NOT believe what I had just done.

Only then did I take into account my surroundings. I was amazed. The place was like a barren wasteland. As far as I could see, the land stretched gray and bare. Just hills and cliffs of jagged gray rock. The sky was dark with menacing thunderclouds, and it was freezing cold. I felt desolate.

I started to worry, because I didn't know in which time period I was, if I was even in North America (a doubtful situation), or, worse, if I was on another planet. I definitely hoped I wasn't. If I was, that would *not* be good. This was really beginning to get ridiculous. First I change my little sister into a bunny out of utter, complete *exasperation*, then I meet this crazy, weird, but nice witch named something like Cleopatra Hipnyza Hishennicus who thinks that she's an Egyptian princess and that little girls use Pantene conditioner and old women have pigtails, *then* I replace mint for lettuce in my attempt to recreate the potion that turned Allie into a bunny, and *then* I get stuck in an unknown location of the universe, in an unknown time period. What had come over me? *WHY* was I acting so incredibly irresponsible? It was simply *blasphemous*! Whatever that word means. I generally have a pretty good vocabulary (big surprise), but that word isn't exactly in it.

As usual, I started thinking about all the terrible things that could happen to me while I was here, *if* I ever escaped. I was in subzero temperatures. I could get hypothermia and die. Aliens could invade. They could take away my magic powers. I could stay here forever and starve to death. Wait, no, that wasn't an option since I could conjure up my own food anyway. But still!

I had driven myself into a frenzy by that point, thinking about all these possible worst-case scenarios. I was so freaked out, in fact, that I began to wonder what was happening to me. Oh no! Was I being possessed? Had an evil wizard possessed me? Had a *Zhawaswhan* (this unbelievable creature I made up, but that's a different story) abducted my common sense straight from my brain, right from under my nose (or rather, *over* my nose)? Had a **GHOST** possessed me and made me do all this crazy stuff?! I figured I was hallucinating when I thought about the **GHOST.** There was simply no other explanation to how I could have gotten such fantastical, hideous, bogus, utterly *unreal* creatures into my poor, little, feverish, frantic head. After all, didn't thinking about *ghosts* prove to some witches to be fatal? Yikes, I'm getting into that rotten subject again. Either way, I had to find something to redirect my brain so I wouldn't end up in the ICU at the hospital (and by the way, ICU means "Intensive Care Unit"), or, worse, in an asylum for demented witches. Hey, shouldn't that crazy witch I just met, Cleo, be in one of those? On second thought, no, she shouldn't be, because she's nice, and nice witches don't normally end up in asylums unless they're drunk, which she most certainly is *not.*

Bummed out at myself, I collapsed into hysterics. I screamed like a psyched fan at a soccer game (I hate soccer) and kicked my legs out in front of me.

Getting control of myself, I started to wonder how to deal with the appalling present situation. What could I do? A potion spell? A reverse incantation spell? That would have helped, but I couldn't use it because I didn't have the original potion. I was in the same circumstance that my poor, poor little sister was in. I was being so irresponsible! Why did this have to happen to me and not to someone else?!

I began to feel lonely, so I murmured a fumbled spell to make a kitten appear that I could play with until I thought of something. Most unfortunately (or fortunately, whichever way you choose to think about it), my spell, as usual, went entirely wrong. Instead of a sweet little kitten, I had on my hands a snow-bank-white flying puppy. It was very energetic and ran around my legs, barking madly. Uh-oh. Much as I loved this creature, there was just no way my mother would allow me to add another animal to our enormous zoo collection at home.

Because in case I didn't inform you earlier, I already had...*only*...three mice, four hamsters, two gerbils, six horses, eight little baby kittens (which I guess I should have brought here instead of trying to create a new one), and sixteen beautiful tropical fish. Not to mention an enchanted bunny rabbit who just so happened to be my sister and now a flying puppy with a white, fuzzy body and lavender wings. *Oh dear.*

I scooped up the furry little thing—it was small enough to be a toy breed—and held it fast in my arms so that it couldn't escape. It licked my face, and I gasped and spluttered. It's probably kind of obvious that I haven't dealt with dogs a whole lot before.

Then it did something weird. After I held it, it squirmed and fell out of my grasp—typical. Then it started pawing at the ground. Immediately, the air took on a glistening, secretly shimmery quality. A pink tunnel appeared. It was just a bubbling, boiling oval of pinkness, but I sure knew what it meant.

I gasped. A travel tunnel...or was it a portal? I'd never seen one in my life. Closing my eyes and taking a deep breath, I stepped right in. The pup jumped into my outstretched hands, looking surprised at my ashen face. I couldn't help it. I laughed. It was just so adorable.

In no time at all, I was back in my living room with the dog licking my face. Makeup drizzled down my cheeks and inky black mascara dropped into my eyes. Ouch! It stung. Bad.

Once my vision cleared, I could see Mom standing there like a phantom. Oh, not a phantom, since that's a—*don't say the word*—GHOST, but maybe a wild caveman going by the stunned, traumatized, utterly flabbergasted look she wore on her face. I would have burst out laughing if it weren't for the animal's life at stake here.

Finally she managed to choke out a few flummoxed words. "Sapphire?" she groaned, rubbing her perplexed forehead. "Is that you?"

I had no time to worry about why my own mom was calling me by my middle name, which I don't even go by (EVER), but I figured it was safe to go with the assumption that she was more than a little discombobulated. "Yeah, it's me," I replied, almost unable to stand erect. "Listen, I know this is confusing, but I can explain."

Dad had come out of the kitchen now. He gaped at me, with his mouth so wide open I could probably see his tonsils (disgusting!).

"Zoey," he gasped when he saw me, "what in the world has HAPPENED to you? And what's that puppy doing here?"

Something had happened to me? I looked down and realized that my new bootcut jeans were tattered, my purple-and-green, waist-length striped hair was a gargantuan mess, and my four-inch wedge heels had gotten lost somewhere in the process.

Oh, I guess I should explain about my hair. I had just wanted it to look like a masterpiece, something truly original, so I decided that purple-and-green striped hair was the best choice to go with my complexion. I guess my friends have gotten used to it by now.

I stared up at Dad and wished the explanation were shorter, so I thought of something quick, and replied, "I think the explanation to the current state of affairs may take longer than is duly intended. Could we finish this conversation later when I'm finished showering, please?"

"No, young lady," Mom stopped me as I began to walk to the door. "You just stop right there. We want to know *exactly* what you got yourself into and *exactly* why you got yourself into it."

I groaned and began with heavy, super-phony melancholy in my voice. "I was time traveling...by accident," I said.

Mom was on alert. "What do you mean...*by accident*?" she demanded.

"Well, it's kind of a long story," I admitted.

"Go on," Dad said.

I cleared my throat and prepared myself for this bold undertaking of explaining myself to my parents. "So," I began, and then I cleared my throat again. And again. And again. "Anyway." I did it again.

Mom and Dad looked like they were prepared to be patient with me. You know, I don't think patience was a character trait they ever needed until I came along.

I decided to talk really fast and get this all over with. "So I wanted to remake the potion for Allie. I knew that it probably wouldn't work; I just wanted to try. And I sort of...*substituted*...a few of the ingredients.

And I guess I made a time travel potion by accident instead."

"And what is that *dog* doing here?" Mom was not going to be Miss Nice Mommy for me anymore.

"Well, I was kind of lonely on that random planet, so I wished for a cuddly friend and got this pup, who created a travel tunnel and then escaped with me," I answered, still babbling hysterically quickly.

"And therefore, am I correct in assuming that you were in a situation that, without that *dog*, could have proven to be fatal?" The tone in which Mom said *dog* wasn't very kind. I hugged the puppy close to protect it from such insults.

"Well, yes, I suppose so," I replied carefully.

Zara Sapphire Williams, you are a riot!" This time it was Dad speaking. "This is ridiculous. I'm glad you escaped from there unharmed. For all we know a pack of vampires or hungry aliens was living on that planet, ready to attack you!"

Um, that whole vampire-alien thing *was* a little farfetched, but I had to admit, it was a possibility. I flipped my hair over my shoulder and sighed guiltily. "I told you already, I got there by accident! I was just trying to help…"

Dad sighed. "Oh, all right, now go take a shower and clean yourself up."

"We will further discuss this—how shall I put it— *abysmal* show of irresponsibility once you are all cleaned up and every unfortunate event has been accounted for," Mom added.

I showered and changed into a magically conjured outfit. I just hated the witchy contemporary clothing store at the Witchland Mall, Abercrombie and Witch!

When I finally came down, I realized I should have put myself into time lapse. Despite trying to hurry with my outfitting, my parents were already seated at the dining table to eat dinner. Now they only had more fire to fuel my scolding.

I stood at the bottom of the stairway, looking at them expectantly. They didn't say anything. This was going to take a while.

Anyway, we just ate dinner in silence. Mashed potatoes and gravy, with witchy ice cream for dessert (that I concocted. Its flavor: a mix of lemon, orange, plum, and this fruit I made up. I still need to figure out what to call it; I'm thinking of Starburst, like the candy). Come to think of it, I was actually surprised that I even *got* to have dessert, considering what I had done that day.

After dessert, Mom took me to her room and announced that her daughter was, "like, way, *way* behind in her witchery studies," and that she could do well with "a whole lot of positive reinforcement." I must say, I agreed with her, though I'd rather be designing and creating dresses than studying witchcraft.

And so of course it happened that I went into time warp and recited different variations of the time travel spell over and over so that if I forgot one, I could use the other. She set some most unnecessary ground rules too, such as me not being allowed to time travel without prior permission. A product of my childish non-rule-following, I suppose.

Eleven

My Little Conversation with Mom

The cousins were coming the next evening, so evidently I needed a meeting with Miss Chief Witch Cleo to resolve the issue. It was Sunday, and we had Memorial Day long weekend as well as a teacher work day, so they'd be here two straight days from Baltimore.

Cleo materialized in my room, as expected, that morning at around ten o'clock. This time, instead of turning her down, I welcomed her, wondering how she always knew what was up with my life.

"Hi," I greeted her.

"Hello, Zoey," she repeated in an extraordinarily focused monotone voice. "Back to business. I will create your sister's clone, but there is one catch to the solution—clones find it terribly difficult to recall much, if any, of their past.

"Therefore," she continued, "you will have to answer for the girl and do your best to redirect the question. Now, let me have her so I can perform the necessary incantations."

I handed her the carrot-guzzling and now chubby bunny Allie so she could do her complicated magic.

I leaned back on my bed lazily. I didn't really care *how* she performed the spell, I just wanted Allie to have her duplicate in time. And not a bunny clone. I wanted to see my sister in person, even *if* she was only the touchable hologram version.

After a tense few minutes of waiting, the experienced witch now had a fully programmed 3-D textured hologram of my little sister. I stared at the model in wonder. It was fully still and not moving a muscle, which, when I think about it, is not terribly surprising because it probably didn't even *have* muscles.

It, or rather *she*, was wearing a strapless, satin, knee-length gown scattered with abstract patterns of sparkles. I smiled as I realized that it was the one I had designed, conjured, and given to Allie for her seventh birthday. I wondered if she had worn it at all in the last month. Probably.

"And now," Cleopatra beamed, "I'll register the incantation necessary to make this clone move freely, then I'll administer the dosage for it to have an adequate IQ and recalling of past, at least enough for it to be an intellectual robot."

She muttered a few more spells, then the duplicate instantaneously began to move. I stared at it for a few seconds, and then it started to talk to me.

"Oh, hi, Zoey!" It spoke in the same overenergetic way that the real Allie did. "I am so, like, UBERexcited to be here with you again, back from being a bunny! That was, like, *soooooo* boring, you just can't imagine how boring it was. I was bored out of my skull! Everyone staring at me like I was the most interesting specimen in the whole big wide gigantic world! Oh, and who is *that*?"

She was pointing to the flying puppy, which I hadn't named yet.

"I saw him earlier today, and I thought he was going to eat me, since I was just a bunny rabbit. Oh, and there's *another* bunny on the other side of the room! It looks just like I did! OMG! It's SOOOOOO CUTE! Can I play with it?"

I stuttered, trying to make up a dozen reasons so that the clone COULDN'T play with it. However, just as I thought of the first one, she literally vanished into thin air. I glared intently at the spot where she'd gone.

"We can't simply sit here and listen to her incessant raving, obviously. We need to practice the drill." I saw Cleo looking down at me most disapprovingly.

"Um, what drill?" I inquired, completely and utterly oblivious to the fact that she was here for a reason and had work to get done.

"Answering for her, of course. Now, what would you say if they asked her how school was going?"

"Um…uh…" I stammered, unable to think of an answer.

She pressed an obnoxious buzzer and asked me again. My mind went blank. *Oh dear.* This was really gonna be one long, drawn-out afternoon.

✳ ✳ ✳

Karen, Krystal, and Kiera came only a few minutes after my new witchy friend, Cleopatra blah-blah-blah, left. They were all very excited about seeing us, and didn't seem to realize at all that they were chatting animatedly with a phony version of my sister. Unfortunately, Mom was not nearly so fooled.

As she served lunch to the guests, she snarled hurried threats and poured out questions into my ears.

"*Zara Sapphire Williams*," she began.

"Caroline, would you pass that delightful-looking summer squash?" my aunt asked, gesturing toward the plate piled high with hideous, squishy, snot-colored vegetables that looked anything but delightful.

Mom made sure to sit next to me during dinner. Paying no attention at all to the ongoing conversations, she hissed at me in a dangerous voice, "*I had planned to tell everyone that Allie went to a special camp for gifted children that only opens once a year, so she had to go right now, no matter how rude it seemed...*"

I stifled a laugh. *Allie?* At a camp for *gifted children*? Nonsense!

"And," she continued, her voice rising by the millisecond, "*you have somehow managed to clone her. You could have gotten hurt in the process! Seriously injured! Killed!*"

"Sorry, Mom, but I really *don't* think—" I began.

"*Zara Sapphire Williams, this will not be without consequences...*" Mom snarled dangerously.

"Do you think so too, Caroline?" my aunt asked abruptly. "We need to make our decision."

Mom looked up, surprised, and she seemed to be wondering what to say. "Oh, yes," she replied at last. "Charming idea...absolutely *charming*..."

"Really?" Kiera said. "You think the idea of going to a slime museum is charming? We all wanted to go, but we thought you hated anything gross or sticky."

"I amend my statement," Mom said frantically. "What I meant was we shouldn't go! It's a simply horrid idea!"

Everyone seemed surprised at her sudden out-burst. She looked bewildered for a moment but then turned back to me and whispered fiercely, *"How did you do that? I thought I heard voices in your room. Did you get help?"*

"Yes," I answered. There was no way out of this. "But you see, I got it from a most reliable source."

"And what was that 'source'?" she questioned, her tone becoming softer, more threatening.

"The head of the witchy community," I answered. It sounded so silly, even to me—*I got help from a complete stranger, who thinks she's a princess and wears pigtails...* "She's nice. She thinks she used to be an Egyptian prin-cess, but her memory's fine, really. And she—Cleo—is going to help me find the cure for my sister."

"Aunt Caroline! I want ice cream!" Karen shouted suddenly.

"You have to say 'please', honey," my aunt scolded.

"Oh—oh, yes, of course, dear," Mom murmured. "How could I have possibly forgotten dessert? It's the most important and nutritious part of the meal."

My cousins laughed, and I did too. Obviously, all of this drama over Allie and that head witch woman was taking its toll on Mom's mind. I only hoped that it was temporary.

Mom became mysteriously quiet afterward. I observed her carefully for any signs that might explain her silence, but the only thing that I could think of was...*did she know Cleopatra?*

✳ ✳ ✳

That first day we had an entire afternoon to ourselves. I introduced my "new pet bunny" to the cousins and informed them that it was named after my sister, Allie. They didn't seem to be suspicious at all! In fact, they loved the whole surprise setup and cooed over "that adorable fuzzy 'wittle' bun-bun-bunny...

After that we went to this cool planetarium called the Terra 66 and watched a show about Europa, one of Jupiter's moons that some people say might have exciting inhabitants. Allie, or rather, should I say her *clone,* didn't act up, even though the thrilling parts of the 3-D, computer-animated movie were pretty breathtaking. I was really surprised. The clone should have Allie's looks as well as her personality.

Once *that* was over, we ate dinner at that Italian pasta & pizza restaurant, Campizzi's. That was where the duplicate's bothersome behavior first started.

I was rather happy when she started acting up, because the fear of someone suspecting something was gnawing at my mind the whole time that she was being good. When the waitress, a stunningly gorgeous Italian girl wearing a scarf and high heels, strutted over to the table, the clone acted all nicey-nicey and asked for macaroni and cheese. Then, just as the waitress turned away, the clone jumped out of her chair and swiftly tore down the ribbon hanging on the back of the girl's waitress-gown-thingamajig. My parents looked horrified even though they knew it was only Allie's *clone,* not really her.

It was sort of funny, really. Not too much, because she was acting up so badly. Oh, all right, I admit...it was absolutely HILARIOUS! Anyway, we had to pay for the waitress's torn gown-thingy since it was a part of her uniform.

After that, we decided to take a "little stroll" in one of the numerous parks in our little city. The park we were going to was called Russell Falls, and it was a huge one with two or three playgrounds. Allie's clone instinctively ran to one of them, aggressively pushed an innocent little girl with pigtails off the swing set, and climbed onto one of the swings (babyish!). The little girl began to cry and clung to her mommy. Our furtive duplicate deviously jumped off the swing she was on, walked to the girl, whose face was still turned away, and tugged at one of her neon pink bows she was wearing so that it also ripped and came off. I didn't know why, but this clone seemed to enjoy ripping ribbons.

The girl cried and wailed even harder. Her mother shot us a dirty look and strutted away with her daughter clinging tightly to her leg.

In all honesty, it was a pretty satisfactory day, except for the misery that the clone brought to her innocuous, helpless victims.

Our guests left on Tuesday at nine in the evening. I heaved a sigh of relief! The last few days had rolled on without any major disasters. I was feeling triumphant because the clone procedure had worked but also depressed because I *still* wasn't sure about how to get my sister back to normal again.

Twelve

The Future?!

I sat down on my bed and enjoyed a grand sulk to clear my mind. I had to think about how to cure Allie. So I held her in my lap and began my intense sulking routine, which, always, for some absurd and unheard-of reason, makes me feel better.

I thought about whether or not some witch, somewhere, had invented a generic reverse incantation potion to work in place of the original spells for all enchantments. Maybe…?! *NOT!* There was absolutely no way someone could've invented reverse incantation for a spell that didn't *have* reverse incantation without the original potion.

I tried to pull out as much immense concentration as I could from the depths of my mind and then loudly chanted a summoning spell to get help. This time I summoned a witchcraft & wizardry rules book from my parents' library. I'd been trying to find this book for years but it was well hidden in the attic where I couldn't get to it. Don't ask me why—my mom has some zany hiding places. Now that I'd learned the summoning spell, I hoped the book would come flying to me. Soon I decided that enough time had elapsed for the spell to take effect and for the book to come to me. I marched downstairs to my parents' bedroom. There, on the bed, was the hardbound book. Actually, it looked more like an old photo album than a book. It was dark brown, with a soft leather cover. The book had little rhinestones dotting the gold border, and the words on the cover were also engraved in slightly faded gold.

Witchcraft Rules

I lugged the huge book up to my room and opened up the "Table of contents and index" page. The book smelled very musty and dusty. I sneezed.

Then I screamed. Three or four very large *moths* fluttered out from within the tattered pages. Haunting music, soft at first, then louder, emanated from the threadbare paper. It reached a crescendo point so loud that I thought my parents had to be able to hear it from downstairs. The volume then went steadily down. I couldn't exactly place what type of music it was. It was scary, definitely; not like the thrill you get while watching a horror movie, but more like the suspense music that goes on while people look for signs of—how should I say it—***paranormal activity***...No, don't say the other word!

After a minute or two of listening to this bizarre *music*, I decided to start looking for what I needed. I wanted to find the section labeled "reverse incantation rules," on page sixty-six. The print was in ancient-looking calligraphy that was exceedingly difficult to read. Just scanning the contents gave me a throbbing headache.

I flipped over to page sixty-six and found a bulleted list of reverse incantation basics. I skimmed down it rapidly. The list took about three pages and made my eyes watery and my vision blurred. Apparently my waterproof mascara *wasn't* as waterproof as Lancôme Paris claimed it was.

Suddenly, I got to a bullet point that just about made me collapse in a heap. In fact, I did find myself rolling off the bed and accidentally kicking my flying puppy after I read it.

It stated that for transformation spells, you *could* create a potion for reversing the enchantment as long as it had the same incantations as the original one. Most unfortunately, however, you needed new ingredients that you could only get in the future. These new ingredients were located at a witchy lab disguised as a library a few hundred miles south of where we live, and a couple hundred years in the future.

I gasped. Who had made the book? It would have been a major breakthrough in witchy chemistry or whatever the subject was if someone had known about it. If my mom had hidden it away in the attic in an aggravating show of secrecy even though she knew I wanted it, she would have had a reason for doing that. I had to show this to you-know-who. Even *she* didn't know about this. If she did, she would have told me by now.

I performed the necessary invocations to summon her (she had taught me last time we met) and witnessed the flurry of diamonds with mounting impatience. I wanted discoveries, and I wanted them *now*!

"OH MY GOSH! LOOK WHAT I FOUND!" I hollered at the breaking point of my lungs' capacity.

"Calm down," Cleo chided. "What did you find? Show me the book. If it's a breakthrough in your sister's enchantment reversing, I need to know."

I turned the book toward her, and she studied the highlighted bullet point. "Wow," she breathed finally, handing the fragile book back to me. "This is truly amazing, and I think we can get you to the future without further discussion. But first, do you have any idea of who might possibly have created this article?"

I shook my head. "No. I wish I did, though. All I know is that my mom hid it away from me in an old compartment in the attic. I've been looking for this book for six years now. I always wanted to study it, because it looked like it could help me, you know, later."

She nodded, understanding. "Oh, I get it. Caroline didn't want you to get to know about this because of the danger it might lead you into. Like it is right now, now that you've found it. What I'm wondering is if an old ancestor of yours created it. I'm thinking your mom's side. Maybe a distant cousin of your aunt's…?"

"No. My cousins aren't witches, I've told you that already. And I took the oath—you know, the one with all that stuff about 'sworn to secrecy.' I can't tell anyone about witchiness unless I want to get into serious trouble with the witchy authorities. Like you," I responded.

"Well, I suppose that means the first priority is to get you to the future, two hundred six point six years from now," the witchy chair told me. "First we transport you to the future, then we get this whole thing of who wrote the article sorted out. And if anyone in your family did write it, then who knows what kinds of other discoveries they may have made."

"We'll be famous!"

"Pretty much."

"The Witchbel Prize will be mine!" (*Evil laugh.*)

"Maybe."

"I'll win the prize trip to the Philippines resort and Queen Mackenzie Island!"

"Quite unlikely."

I rolled my eyes. "Well, at least we'll be famous," I mouthed to my dog and Allie.

She smiled at me. "And now," she said, "I'll be transporting you to the place you need to go to. One, two, three—"

"NO!" I interjected quickly. "First I need to know, like, what to do and stuff. Like, where I'm gonna go, and what I'm gonna do there. And stuff."

"Oh, yes," she said, looking surprised at herself. "Of course. I always seem to forget what I'm saying of late. Rapid aging, I suppose. Did you know that lotion containing coconut oil helps in slowing down the process of aging?"

"You're getting way off track again," I reminded her.

"Oh, yes, of course! I simply *must* remember what I'm saying. I must be making such an awful impression right now! Do you have any tips on how to make decent conversation with highly heralded, witchy politicians while keeping track of all other areas of the brain?"

I groaned strenuously. "Look, this conversation is currently getting, like, waaaaaay out of hand over here. So, anyhow, let's get back to the point that we were discussing, um, earlier. Like you were saying, how am I going to get there, and what am I supposed to do when I *do* get there?"

"First of all, what I'm dying to know is—wait, I most certainly do not mean dying as literally dying. I am simply telling you this because little children sometimes get scared at the mere mention of such a grim prospect as death. And please note that I am not implying that you are little. In fact, I hardly believe that a twelve-year-old girl should qualify as juvenile—" the witch began.

"OMG!" I cut her off with a frustrated cry. "I am not twelve years old; I am thirteen. And even if that was significantly pertinent information, I would not give it much thought if I were you. Just ask what you wanted to ask and let's be done with this whole operation."

"Oh dear, I *am* sorry! As I was saying before I got so terribly wildly off track, as is a habit with me now—just like ditching the Pantene—"

"Oh wooooooow!" I shook my head in irritation. "Listen, I know this whole thing about traveling to the future is exciting, but you need to be more focused. And I say this because I want to cure my sister," I added hastily.

"I am so sorry! Think, brain, think! What is it that you were wanting to inquire about just now?!" the witch cried, now almost as exasperated with herself as I was.

"About…um…something that you were *dying* to know…" my voice trailed off.

"Oh, yes! About the potion. You know, the original thing. *Where* did you say you got it from? I can't seem to remember whether or not you informed me earlier."

This question caught me off guard. I didn't know what to say. I couldn't tell her about the magic cupboard, could I? I would end up getting in so much trouble! I started to think of an answer when the most-unfortunately-very-smart witch thought of something.

"Did you find it in your kitchen by any chance? I commissioned the witchery workers to create the infrastructure for those contraptions just last month. I had meant for those cupboards to be of help. I never knew they would cause such problems."

"Yes, I know. *I* never knew they could cause such problems, either," I responded icily.

"Ahh, mutuality—my favorite feeling." The witch grinned in satisfaction. "Back to the point. Now, the witchy headquarters in which they discover the reverse incantation spell, two hundred six point six years in the future, is located three hundred or so miles south of the city. You will, however, have to pass through an evil wizard's domain to get there. The HQ is guarded by a magic firewall and a wide range of magic traps—very difficult to pass through without crossing the cursed chemistry lab before it."

I sighed. So much for my implorations for her to remain on track. "Look, I have this vague feeling that evil wizards don't exist. Like…y'know…*polter-geists*…" I murmured inaudibly. My own lone mention of *ghouls* was taking its severe toll on me.

"You need to get a good idea of what exists and what doesn't, Zoey," my witchy friend scolded me. "Evil wizards and Egyptian princesses/mummies… they exist. *Apparitions*…they don't." She staggered backward at her own mention of **GHOSTS**…or should I say, *manifestations*. But I figured it was just a natural side effect of thinking of the *phantasms*, so I left her alone.

Once she regained her center of gravity and balance, she continued, "That's all I'm going to tell you. I don't, in fact, know more than that about the place. But it should be enough. And if I were you, I would enlist another witch's help. Preferably one with a better memory than I have presently. I am terribly sorry about it, but I simply don't know *if* I've even been the slightest bit of help in your endeavors. Perhaps I should have given you a more mentally stable witch for your side of the explorations. Because, to tell you the truth, I barely have enough time to—"

"You've helped me. A lot," I assured her. "So when do I begin the mission? Shouldn't I take a suitcase with me, containing, oh, I don't know, perhaps an extra change of clothes, more acrylic nails, and a backup case of makeup in case of emergencies?" I stuttered.

"There's no time for packing!" she exclaimed. "I will transport you there right now. Your parents have been informed and are terribly tense to have learned about your mission. Especially your mother. Now hurry up and go! There's no need to take Allie with you. But I would recommend that you take that pup, and per-haps your passport, for protection," she added.

"What? I can't go now!" I stammered, collapsing into hysterics. "No way! I'll die! I'll be devoured! I'll be caught by the evil wizard-scientist person! I'll be eaten by a saber-toothed dragon!"

The witch laughed. "No, you won't," she said. "I can guarantee you that. Although I think—let's see—I think there may still be a few species of hypnotic, saber-toothed dragons living in the forest that sur-rounds the witchy HQ..."

"You never told me there was a forest!" I hollered.

Too late.

The room was already starting to spin. I clutched the travel-tunnel puppy in my arms as beautiful galax-ies and nebulae whizzed around me in a striking whirl-wind of lights and color.

✳ ✳ ✳

Part 2

Thirteen

A Hobo from the Seventeenth Century BC

I landed in a conservative-looking, ranch-style-housing neighborhood nestled in some small city in South Dakota. Picturesque houses made of various rich stones and dating all the way back to circa 2026 (that's still in the future for me!) dotted the weaving curb and street line. I stared at the glossy, glassy-looking road. No cars moved across it. Not even high-tech vehicles. This really was the twenty-third or so century.

The houses surprised me, though. I stood on the glassy sidewalk, staring at them and wondering why they didn't look more new-worldish. The air felt smoky and cool. Autumn, I guessed. I teetered on my high-heeled boots.

I just stood there on the sidewalk, picking up my little, cute sapphires, taking in everything, wondering, and wishing for help. I wished I had paid more attention when Mom taught me that force field spell to protect me. I had no idea what to do, or how to do it.

Suddenly, out of nowhere, a girl appeared and knocked me right down over. I rubbed my knee where it hurt.

"Hey, watch it!" she scolded scornfully.

"S-sorry," I stammered, getting up and brushing off my dress.

The girl eyed me suspiciously. I took her in completely.

She was wearing a black dress with abstract, silver sequin patterns all over it. They shone differently depending on the direction of the sunlight. On top of that, around her hips, she had on a clear belt with a tiny, LED-lit screen in the middle. It was blank. I wondered what it was for. Her shoes were silver flats with rhinestones dotting the edges. Nothing special about those, unless you consider how absolutely d-i-v-i-n-e they were.

"Moldy cheese," she muttered, flipping her straight blond hair over her shoulder. "It's a hobo from the seventeenth century BC. And it has a mutilated hedgehog in its arms."

She had a mysteriously attractive accent, sort of a mix of British with a hint of Romanian. I stared at her vengefully, silently firing insults at her in my brain. Who did she think she was? Well, she probably thought that she was a stunning and gorgeous diva, but that was beside the point...though it *was* extremely debatable. I was nowhere *near* a hobo from the seventeenth century BC, and my flying puppy, whom I'd begun calling Velvet, was most definitely *not* a mutilated hedgehog, or a deformed one!

"I'm not a hobo, you dummy," I defended myself. "And this is my *dog*. NOT a mutilated hedgehog."

"It speaks!" she exclaimed in a very unkind tone of mock surprise. "Where's your passport? You can't just come here without one. It's the law. You know, bill sixteen twenty-one, passed two months ago?"

I most certainly did *not* know what bill 1621 was, but I wasn't about to let her know that, so I calmly took out my passport (good thing I brought it) and handed it to her. She flipped the pages easily with her super-long, glossy nails. A confused look took over her face.

"Where are the TSHs?" she demanded.

"What are TSHs?" I inquired, giving in.

"Touch-screen holograms, you hobo. Every modern-day passport has them. That was after pass-ports were stored on QPC—as in *quantum personal computer*—hard drives, but that became too much inconvenience. So I guess I was right about you being a hobo from the seventeenth century BC. Tough luck around here!"

I gasped, tempted to do something violent with her. "Listen," I began in a snotty tone. "Just because I'm not from here doesn't mean you have the right to act like this with me. I may not have a touch-screen hologram passport, but that doesn't give you the right to—"

Apparently saying this was enough for the girl to want to kidnap me, or at least something like that. She whipped out a small, iPhone-like thing, and without even dialing, she shouted into it, "Robot three eighty-four. Driver. Access mode forty-six. Rapid action."

Out of nowhere, a car—or was it a rocket?—mate-rialized with a human-sized robot creature in the front seat. The car was a mixture of many vehicles. It was huge and had a bike rack at the back. There were four rows with three seats each, each with its own unique features. The rocket car had fiery jets at the back and looked as if some mad scientist had created it (and I really wouldn't be surprised if it had been made by a mad scientist).

From the front seat, the robot driver got out. It had metal plates and buckles covering its mechanical body from head to foot (it didn't have toes). I just stood there with my mouth wide open. I had never seen anything so cool or high tech before.

The robot advanced toward me and picked me up with a blood circulation-cutting grasp. I struggled, but it was too strong and hefty. Before I knew it, I was being tossed into the seat beside it.

The girl grinned wickedly and slid gracefully into the seat next to mine. I squirmed uncomfortably, trying to look back at the other three rows of seats and see what cool features they had.

I managed to turn myself 180 degrees by the time the vehicle moved off. From here, I could see the three rows behind me. The second one had three teeny screens on trays attached to the seats. Curious, I pressed a 3-D button on one of them. I expected to see some TSH or animated movie pop up, but instead there came an animated picture of a cascading waterfall in motion.

I felt sharp, manicured nails grab me and pull me back from my position. I swung around to face my evil captor, who was, incidentally, just a kid and looked like a gorgeous teen supermodel.

"So you think you're so smart, huh?" she demanded accusingly. I shook my head meekly.

"Oh yes you do! But you don't know anything! You're coming here randomly, without anyone accompanying you, disguised as a *hobo*!

"And what's more," she continued menacingly as the vehicle zoomed past more and more glossy streets, "you won't find lodging anywhere here. I have a house to get to and a police station to report you to, and I know more about you than you think. I know you're not from here, and I know you've time traveled to get here. And since we have not yet succeeded in inventing time travel, you must be either from the near future—in which case you might be of help around here—or you are from the past and have somehow succeeded in getting here, which I will investigate later."

I gulped. She *did* know more than I'd expected, and it was beginning to worry me.

To get away from her incessant threats, I twisted around some more to check out the remaining three rows. This time, my captor made no attempt to keep me from doing so. Progress.

The second row contained amenities and nothing else. Necessary possessions decorated the windowsills.

The next row of seats included nothing special except for—was that a *chemical transporter*?! I had only seen stuff like this in science fiction movies! It was just a little metal platform next to one of the seats, but the air shone and glimmered strangely above it.

The last row was also interesting.

The walls here had all sorts of screens filling up their originally blank space. Some of them were big enough to be flat-screen television sets, but most of them ranged in size from the screen of an iPad to the screen of a Galaxy S4 to the screen of an iPod Nano.

Two or three of the larger screens had holograms floating around on them. They were of various different pictures. Some of them had backgrounds (i.e., landscaping or flowers), and others were simply colorful geometrical designs.

I was absolutely captivated. Besides being a fashion designer, I also like science, and I was starting to work out the mechanics of how those could work. I'd never even seen a 3-D hologram before, least of all an entire museum of touch screen ones.

Finally, we stopped at a street looking no different from the ones I'd seen before now. The robot forcefully pushed me out of the rocket car. The girl led me up the rich-looking, ruby red steps to what must have been her house. It became clear that we were not going to the police station.

She let go of my hand at the door. I rubbed my hand, glad to be rid of her steely grip and to have my circulation back.

Then I paid attention to the door. It looked so high tech! There was no lock on the door, so she didn't use keys. Instead, there was a voice-recognition box and a fingerprinting system to allow visitors in. The girl mumbled the password, and the door swung open with ease.

She led me into the front hall, and I walked along with her, rendered speechless. The front hall alone was nothing even vaguely resembling ordinary. Aside from the TSHs decorating the walls, there was also the air quality. It was exceedingly shimmery and made me suspicious. Stray holograms featuring flowers, shapes, and various other things floated through it. Occasionally, a rocket hologram would whiz through the air. The background colors and designs on the walls were continuously shifting and changing. It was beautiful.

After the front hall came the living area. This was much simpler. It was decorated in classic style, with elegant, cherry wood bookshelves and white couches and loveseats. It looked very ordinary to me. Not a single thing about it was surprising.

I silently followed her into the kitchen. I had no time to notice the décor there, because as soon as we entered, a stylish lady wearing lots of makeup, long gel nails, and a very skeptical expression came in.

"Hi, Mom! I'm home!" the girl shouted with an unusually kind tone of voice.

"Hi, Jenny," the girl's mom replied, sounding tired. "Who have you kidnapped now?"

Jenny looked unnecessarily offended. "You know I've never kidnapped anyone before," she lied bluntly.

"Then who's that with you?" her mom retorted.

"Mom, this is my friend. I don't know her name yet. I met her earlier; she was staring at the sidewalk like a disoriented hobo or something. She's time traveled to get here from about two hundred years in the past. She needs lodging overnight, preferably in the conference room so we can figure out what the issue is. She's a witch."

Fourteen

Two Hundred Years into the Future

Well, I just about fell completely over when I heard her make that announcement. I sputtered and stammered and stuttered, attempting to look composed while demanding an explanation.

Jenny laughed, but it was no longer a wicked laugh. "I'm sorry. I knew all along that you were a witch—how could I not? It was so obvious! How else could you be in this part of the country and not know what a 3-D hologram looks like, not have a robot, let yourself get kidnapped, and look confident the whole time?"

I looked into her icy blue eyes and realized that she wasn't lying. "But how come you were so mean?" I asked, still flustered.

"I had to get you to safety, didn't I?" she demanded. "You would've been suspicious if I hadn't gotten you under control. It was for your own good. Trust me, I've done this kind of thing before. I just need to know what the issue is, and we can get it solved."

I took a deep breath. "It's not that simple," I informed her. "I have to go through the chemistry lab, through the forest, break through the firewall, and get to the witchy headquarters."

Jenny still looked bewildered. "But *why*?!" she almost yelled. "Why the heck would you want to do something like that? It's *unreal!*"

"Because I changed my sister into a bunny and can't get back the original potion that seeped into the tiles, and I discovered in a hidden book that the reverse incantation potion would be discovered now, and I need to get past all those things to reverse the enchantment," I offered in explanation.

Jenny shook her head. "That's ridiculous!"

"I know," I agreed quietly. "Thank you for agreeing to help me."

"Anyway, first we need to at least know what to call each other. What's your name, anyway?" Jenny inquired.

"Zoey," I answered. "But my mom seems to think that I was christened Zara."

"So we both have unusual names. At least yours is pretty. Moldy cheese, I can't imagine how Mom came up with mine."

Jenny's mother, who had been listening to the exchange in rapt attention and looking both amused and worried, now scolded her daughter. "We chose that name because we thought it was unique," she reprimanded. "And it *is* pretty. Jennifer is a beautiful name."

Jenny rolled her eyes. "Nice going, Mom. Well, anyway, *Zoey*, let me take you up to the conference room and map out our route. This won't be easy, I'm telling you right now. But if you're willing to risk it, so am I."

"Where is the conference room?" I questioned, following her out of the room.

"Wait a minute," Jenny's mom said, stopping us. "You must be starving, Zoey. Jenny, take what you want from the pantry and install Zoey's voice on the voice-recognition box. She's going to need it."

After all of this was said and done, Jenny took me to the elevator (seriously! An *elevator* in a house!) and told the doors to open. We strolled in. I glanced at the wall and then fixed my eyes onto it.

Jenny noticed my intense gazes. "Oh, *those*," she giggled. "I see what you're looking at. The holograms aren't touch screen. They just show you pictures of the rooms."

On each elevator button was a projected hologram showing an image of each different room. "Tell it where you want it to go. See for yourself the wonders of high-tech devices," Jenny instructed in a scholarly tone.

"Go to the conference room on the third and top floor," I told the elevator.

"Elevator transporting guests to conference room," a Siri-like, female voice replied.

Soon, we were in a room with another classic-style, cherry wood table and matching chairs to go along with it. The walls of this room were free of holograms and screens, but the table was positively drenched in them. I munched on lemon-flavored, star-shaped Oreos and marshmallows while Jenny set up the projector board.

Soon, everything was ready. Jenny projected what looked like an animated hologram of a map onto the wall.

"That's the route that we need to map out," she expounded. She then instructed the map in a mechanical voice, "Show us route three twenty-one to get from our property to the witchy HQ premises."

The map immediately zoomed in to a highlighted route, shown in neon pink on the wall. I gazed at it, impressed.

"The route cuts through the witchy chemistry lab, owned by that stupid, deranged, selfish scientist," Jenny proclaimed. "We go through the entryway here, then we have to go through some conference rooms, then through a multipurpose hall. After that, we can cut through the actual main lab while no one's in there, go out through the exit, and be done with it."

I shook my head. "That's too hard," I complained.

"Well, you've gotta do it if you want to reverse your sister's enchantment," Jenny said, ignoring me. "After you cut through the actual lab and get to the exit, you will be faced with the forest," she continued, scrolling up the pathway with her remote. "Here, you simply have to go straight through a whole lot of miles of thick greenery, walking."

"That part will be easy," I remarked.

"Not quite. Don't you know about the hypnotic, saber-toothed dragons?"

My jaw dropped. "So those *are* real, after all," I groaned. "Will they kill us? Eat us? What will they do?"

"Nothing. But they'll steal our food supply," Jenny replied. "We'll have to hide that, or else it won't be long before we starve."

"Can't you just conjure up more food for us?" I questioned.

Jenny gave me a weird look. "Your mother didn't make you study witchery much, did she? What about spell technique and skills, and rules?"

"She did!" I answered quickly. "I just didn't pay any attention, that's all. Must be the same for you."

Jenny nodded, understanding, and then explained, "Your magic goes away once you enter that forest. You're powerless."

"Oh," I murmured, discouraged by this new information.

"After that," she continued, "you're free to enter the witchy HQ, as long as you have proof of being a witch. All the proof you need, really, is to show them some of your magic. Unless you've been there before, like me. Then you just have to undergo voice recognition and this fingerprinting test that they do."

"I thought there was a firewall, whatever that is, or something," I countered.

"You break through that firewall if you manage to pass through the forest," Jenny explained.

"That's cool! So now, basically all I have to do is to get the potion, say bye to everyone, and get home?" I shouted.

"Exactly!" she replied.

"Awesome!"

"But it's gonna be harder than you think."

"Thank you for being most encouraging and optimistic," I said dryly.

We took the elevator back down and met Jenny's mother in the kitchen, which I now noticed held appliances that I had never seen before. She smiled at us. "So how is your little mission going?" she inquired.

"It's not *little*, Mom," Jenny corrected.

"I thought so. When are you guys leaving? I need you to be back by the end of the day, and don't go past that old, famous Starbucks ruin near the community shopping center. I grant that you two are trustable and will not enter the forest, but it's safe to have backup just in case."

Jenny winked at me. "You're right. We're not entering the forest," she fibbed, without flinching. "We know about the magic firewall and the saber-toothed dragons and all that. But we'll need food to take with us, and a little extra, you know, in case the dragons get it."

"So you *are* entering the forest," her mom said. Jenny covered her mouth and turned a sheepish grin on me, realizing what she'd just said. I frowned at her.

"Well, in that case, you two are simply not going on the mission, whatever it is," she snapped. "Zoey, I'm sorry about this, but I really can't allow my daughter to go there alone. There must be an alternative."

"B-but there isn't!" Jenny squeaked. "We have to reverse her sister's enchantment! Have I ever come back from a mission hurt, other than a few scrapes, bruises, and chipped nails?"

"It's fine. Really," I purred soothingly, giving in. I scratched Jenny to warn her not to say anything.

"Anyway, neither of you are going anywhere, so now why don't you summon your robot and drop this witch off wherever she lives?" Jenny's mom asked nicely.

Jenny looked worried, like she had no idea what to do.

"Is there a way to confuse your mom into thinking that we're not going anywhere dangerous?" I whispered.

"Oh yes, there is, if you can go bring me some powdered mermaid scales and sterilized unicorn silk to make a potion," Jenny said. "Which, in the current circumstances, is SO not going to happen."

I thought about the books that I'd read while desperately searching for a cure for my sister. Did any of them have something about confusing jinxes? Why hadn't I paid better attention? But there just had to be some way to do this…They didn't make such time-consuming reading material for no reason whatsoever…or did they?

Then I thought of something. The ancient Mystifying Mist, which could be conjured by a very simple incantation. As far as I had read, it hadn't been used in nearly half a century. But it would work now. It had to.

Most unfortunately, to get the full force of this normally flimsy spell, you had to break something.

"*Mystify!*" I yelled, looking around for something preferably inexpensive that I could break.

The only thing in sight that wasn't exquisitely painted was a translucent glass contraption sitting on a nearby countertop. I seized it guiltily and flung it onto the tiled floor.

Jenny's mother's disapproving expression suddenly turned to one of shock and dismay. "AAAAAAHHH-HHH! My new mixoscope!" she screamed hysterically. The spell had worked, but the consequences weren't exactly what you'd call *reassuring.*

Jenny and I exchanged panicked glances, and then we both instinctively ran for it. We didn't stop to catch our breath until we had reached the top floor of her gigantic manor.

"*What did you have to do that for?*" she demanded angrily, panting.

"What did I do *what* for?" I asked innocently.

"That was, like, the lamest bewilderment charm *ever*! It'll wear off in two *hours!*"

I smiled. "That's not a problem," I announced. "We're sneaking out at night."

A naughty smile crept across Jenny's face. "Yeah," she agreed. "I guess I underestimated your still-very-low intelligence level. We'll go out at nightfall and find somewhere to stay for the night. It's too dangerous to go out past sunset when you're trying to sneak into an evil wizard's domain. There'll be guards and video cameras stationed everywhere."

"All right," I resolved. "But won't your mom be worried?"

"If you're going to worry about that, then I recommend that you think of a plausible solution yourself. I'll leave her a note," Jenny responded. "She'll be mad, but we can't help that, can we? It's more important to reverse your sister's enchantment."

"Oh yeah," I said, suddenly remembering something, "does Starbucks really still exist?"

"As a matter of fact, it does! About three hundred years old, and with all of the modern technology around, it's a miracle that the building's still standing. Our town is famous for it, although everyone says it will fall within the next year. Hobos were horrible at building things—no self-supporting beams or *anything*! But I don't want it to fall—it's the only thing anyone comes to our silly little city for. Apart from the flying skateboards, of course. Just press a button and they fly! No wings needed!" she exclaimed excitedly.

"How charming," I said meekly.

"*Charming*? Isn't that a major hobo adjective?"

I ignored her and tried to muster a smile. "So when do we start packing?"

Fifteen

Malfunctioning Holograms

Jenny did not look happy. My incantation had gone seriously wrong, and now ugly green gloop was splattered all over the walls. "We—you—will have to clean this hot mess up right now," she snapped firmly.

I glanced nervously at the clock. "We don't have much time." But I cleaned it up anyway.

Jenny chanted something complicated under her breath. Her long hair swirled in rapid whirlpools of straightened silk. And then, in front of her, a whole bunch of food appeared, most of it movie theater junk like pizza and popcorn. She scribbled a list of the items and magically stuck the list onto her desk.

"We can eat whatever we want now. This is going to be great, which is mainly the reason that I'm helping you," Jenny said. "We'll bundle this up and carry it together. Or maybe we can shrink it to miniature size and put in our purses."

"That is a lot of junk food," I said.

Jenny scribbled a note on a scrap piece of paper.

Mom: I can't believe I'm actually saying sorry to someone for the first time in my life, but I guess I am. We had to go. OK, OK, sorry! We should be back in about a week, presuming we haven't been drenched in Germ Potion by an evil wizard or enchanted by dragons by then. To see what we took with us, check the list in our rooms; although to be honest, I DON'T recommend that you do! You'll probably faint and what will you do if I'm not here to pour freezing potions on your head to wake you up? Or take away your mascara to wake you up? Whenever I take any of your things, you can always smell it from about sixteen hundred thousand kilometers away, or actually only about one room away, but that's beside the point...

"Be done with it!" I exclaimed impatiently. "*Honestly*, how long can it possibly take you to write a little note? And don't give your mom false information; what if it takes even *more* than a week? Besides, I have a feeling that we'll probably be dealing with plenty of formidable dragons on the way."

✳ ✳ ✳

Jenny groaned when we reached the door. "I forgot to install your voice on the voice-recognition box," she whispered. "I'll have to do it now. I'll set it to 'whisper,' so you don't wake my mom up. My dad doesn't live with us—they're divorced. It's eleven already. I have a feeling that we probably *won't* be getting any lodging for tonight anyway."

I nodded. The voice-recognition version of Siri instructed me to repeat a few phrases after it. Suddenly a touchable rose hologram whizzed by the motion detector and upset the recognition. The automatic mechanical voice apologized. "Sorry, I didn't get that."

"NO!" Jenny gasped as yet another animated waterfall hologram nearly made the motion detector release the alarm. "There must be something wrong with the holograms today! They're not supposed to act like this!"

I caught a textured, mechanically generated flower in my hands while attempting to receive yet another one in hopes of keeping it from interrupting the motion detector and voice-recognition box.

"It won't work if they keep intercepting the signals. Everything's interconnected," Jenny explained gloomily.

I sighed. "Will the recognition box respond if we yell at it? The signals will be stronger than before," I suggested.

"It'll be worth trying." Jenny agreed uneasily. "But Mom is definitely going to wake up if she hears us shouting, so we'll have to run. *Fast!*"

I shouted the phrases that I was supposed to repeat in whispers. At the last one, Jenny's mother came rushing to the front door to see what was happening to her daughter.

We didn't take any looks backward as the door burst open and we fled out of it. Jenny forcefully closed it behind her with an appalling loud crash. It sounded like a sonic boom.

We dashed blindly out over her yard and into the darkness.

"Where's the castle, anyway?" I panted.

"It's not a castle. It's just a huge building," she replied, slowing down. "It's about three miles north of my house. I don't know the exact route, but we can figure that out using my DSX."

"What does DSX stand for?" I questioned further.

Jenny shrugged. "Who knows? The good news is, I have it. The bad news is, it isn't charged. So you'll have to wait awhile during the chanting incantation period."

While I waited, I changed the boring gray street into a hot pink whirlpool.

After a few minutes, Jenny got up. "Here," she said, "it's ready." She spoke into the device, which was just the tiny LED-lit screen she had attached to her belt. "Teleport us from my house to the evil wizard's lab north of here, please."

We materialized in my usual shower of little, cute, miniature sapphires and silver sparkles and Jenny's shower of snowflakes. I felt disoriented and discombobulated.

"W-where are we?" I stuttered.

"We're at the chemistry lab, remember?" Jenny replied. "But we're not going in. We're camping in the courtyard overnight, or for the couple of remaining hours of night."

"Oh yeah," I recalled, still woozy. "How do we get in? Why can't we just teleport ourselves to the other side of the building?"

"We can't teleport ourselves because the teleportation signals will be intercepted by this huge building. And even if they *aren't* intercepted, our magic goes away in the forest, so we can't materialize there," Jenny explained. Even I could tell she was trying to be patient but not succeeding very well.

"I thought teleportation was technology, not magic," I muttered shakily.

"It is technology, but it's not exactly available to the public yet...too expensive."

I wobbled a little and then managed to take a few steps on my own. Jenny steadied me, and we walked to an unenclosed courtyard on the south side of the building.

"It looks like you're free to enter, but you're not. There's an invisible wall. Don't try to go in. You'll only hurt yourself with trying," Jenny cautioned.

"Then how do we get in?" I groaned. This was way more complicated than I'd predicted that it would be.

"More teleportation," she announced.

I grunted.

As we materialized in the courtyard, I pulled a sleeping bag out of thin air while Jenny waved a force field over us to protect us from further invasions. After a quick snack of chocolate-covered marshmallows, we lay down to sleep. I couldn't sleep, though.

Sixteen

Firewall

Dawn broke over the courtyard. Cotton candy-colored clouds drifted across the clear, peach-colored sky. And smudged mascara drizzled down my cheeks.

"Get up, slowpoke," Jenny instructed authoritatively, nudging me. She brushed strands of purple-and-green hair out of my eyes. They fluttered in the light, pleasant morning breeze.

"Well sorry," I shot back groggily. "Just because I'm at your house doesn't mean—wait, where am I?"

"You're in the courtyard, where I just teleported you to. And we have to go through that building undetected," she responded, gesturing to the gracious, secluded chemistry lab.

"Darn it," I muttered. "Then why does the sky look like I'm vacationing in Honolulu?"

"I can say the spell for dark thunderclouds and lightning if it will help in improving your mood," Jenny grumbled sarcastically, my irritation rubbing off on her. "And by the way, Honolulu isn't part of the United States anymore; the French invaded it twenty years ago."

"*Don't do that*," I said, getting out and murmuring spells under my breath. The sleeping bag slowly folded itself up, rolled itself up, shrunk, and hopped into my purse. I stared at the impressive building in front of me. It was absolutely gigantic! It was made out of some glassy material and had rows of windows climbing up to the roof. Pink clouds were swirling at the top of it.

"We should go now," Jenny advised. "We don't need breakfast. Follow me to the entryway to the building. It's very isolated."

I grabbed her arm. "What if there are guards or video cameras?" I demanded, a panicked look on my face.

"Oh yeah!" she said, remembering. "Thanks for reminding me!"

She clapped her hands three times, whistled once, and stomped hard four times. Immediately she disappeared.

I gasped. "Jenny, what are doing?! That invisibility spell is only to be used by witchy college graduates, *remember*?"

"Not if you're ahead in your witchery studies," she contradicted. "Like me. And after I turn you invisible as well, I need you to remember the rules. I'm only fourteen and my invisibility spell won't last if you fall, trip, bump into something, or do anything dumb like that. My protective force field has worn off too, and I can't replenish a major spell like that until two days later because of my age. You do know that, don't you?"

I nodded even though I *didn't* know it. And before I could blink, I had also become indiscernible. Jenny had me hold tightly on to her as she led me to the entrance.

The entrance to the laboratory was located on the south side of the building where we were. She was definitely right when she said it was secluded. Nestled underneath a thick, ten-foot-high briar bush was a white door with two adjoining walls of glassy material on either side. At the top of the door, almost infinitesimally sized, were two tiny LED-lit screens.

"They're not what you think they are," Jenny whispered. "They're not DSXs. They're disguised video cameras, and we can't talk with them around."

I almost fainted as the two LED-lit screens turned around on miniscule mechanical arms sensing our voices. Jenny pulled me away from the door frantically.

She risked chanting soft, quiet spells as we stood about ten feet away from the door. I wondered if there were motion sensors.

After almost a full minute of chanting incantations, Jenny was beginning to become frustrated. "Moldy cheese, the darned thing won't open," she whispered. "There's a firewall. We'll have to risk teleportation into the building. If the signals are intercepted, the motion sensors will catch us."

"There are motion sensors?" I asked, scared. I was still sort of recovering from the shock of the terribly horrifying fact that evil wizard scientists actually *existed.*

"Yes, but being invisible weakens the signals automatically. If there was no firewall, getting in would be easy."

I nodded my understanding. Jenny pushed a few buttons on her DSX, and soon I was materializing and picking up little, cute, miniature sapphires from the floor.

Then it hit me HARD like six hundred thousand of those toy brick walls Allie used to make when she was little: *the stuff that we were carrying* wasn't *invisible!*

I grabbed Jenny's arm forcefully and informed her about the miserable and dire circumstances (sorry, but being melodramatic is sort of a habit with me now). She looked like she was about to have a conniption.

She furiously chanted and stamped her feet and clapped, but sure enough, before I could even take note of my surroundings, the motion sensors and LED cameras were turning and beeping.

We dashed out of the room, which just so happened to be a conference room with the table and walls covered with touch-screen holograms, and into a minor laboratory looking off the doorway. It was filled to overflowing with vials and tubes of weird-colored potions, complex glass contraptions, and hundreds of other things that I would have just LOOOOOOVED to investigate but simply didn't have the chance to do so. We ran around the tables frantically, looking for a place to hide, when...

Crash! Smash!

Jenny, irresponsibly breaking and disobeying her own ground rules, smashed into a table and sent a vial of sea-turquoise potion and a glass contraption quite literally flying through the air. She fell to the ground along with the potion, which splattered all over her. She became visible immediately. I noticed that she also swallowed a drop or two of the potion. I hoped it wasn't anything harmful.

However, I had other things on my mind at that moment. Velvet, worried and freaked out by all the sudden commotion, was barking madly. This, combined with the violent crash, sent the assistant workers or whoever they were of that annoying evil scientist dashing into the room as fast as they could.

✳ ✳ ✳

The door swung open. At the last moment, Jenny picked herself up and hid behind a large screen with me. We couldn't see in front of the screen. It was opaque.

A whole bunch of men in lab coats of different colors—mostly past the human spectrum—swarmed around the broken vial, contraption, and potion. The potion steamed and bubbled on the ground. Jenny looked spaced out and she seemed to be wondering where she was. Not alert and worried, like me.

I couldn't hear what those creepy men were saying, but suddenly one of them shouted something and tore back the screen. From their point of view, some random, spaced-out girl had just appeared, had somehow been able to actually get *into* the building, and was now scheming on completely destroying their laboratory.

One of them picked Jenny up roughly and hailed her out of the room. I followed her like a translucent— *don't say the word…*um…*SPECTER…!*

Velvet, ever the well-behaved puppy, was thankfully quiet. Well, except for the part where Jenny spilled the potion.

Jenny was carried through quite a few rooms. Most of them were conference rooms with the TSHs covering the walls and tables, but some were other minor labs with really cool appliances in them.

For instance, one of the labs had the shimmery air quality that signaled magic was being conducted, and the vials all had multicolored steam coming out of them. Eventually the steam filled the room and changed into different smells: red for raspberries, orange for oranges, yellow for lemons, green for green apple, blue for blueberries, purple for grapes, pink for strawberries, and so on and so forth. Suddenly, everything the steam or vapors touched turned invisible. I think it had something to do with increasing the strength and/or length of invisibility spells.

This happened to be the last room we went into. In the next room, which was just a bare room with a table and a couple of chairs and nothing else, one of the men pushed Jenny into a transparent contraption. It was made up of four walls, eight video cameras, and two motion sensors. The walls glimmered silverish with strong magic.

I followed Jenny into the contraption as the men opened the door. Jenny's face had a perplexed expression on it. She didn't kick, punch, scratch, hit the men, or fight back in any way like I'd have expected her to with her personality. Instead, she just gave in and let the men force her through. I was confounded.

As soon as the men left the room to report to their boss or whoever he was, I shook Jenny to get her back to her senses. It had no effect on her whatsoever. I was beginning to get really worried and freaked out by now.

"Jenny!" I almost shouted, forgetting about the two motion sensors and the video cameras stationed everywhere. "What happened?! You look like a PHANTOM! No, worse, you look like a GHOST!"

The last two sentences had some effect, at least, although saying them almost made me convulse with fear. Jenny's head jerked up with a rough jolt. Her icy blue eyes, which had been misted over, flashed at me in annoyance.

"It's the hobo! The hobo from the seventeenth century BC! With the mutilated, deformed hedgehog!" she hollered.

The cameras beeped, causing me to lose all hope of getting through the building before nightfall. This time, however, not a single witch came in. I guess they thought there was no way of escape from this magical firewall.

Evidently, I needed better tactics in order to get Jenny back her common sense, and perhaps even her memory. She would have been able to help me get out of the contraption if it hadn't been for her current state. It suddenly occurred to me that it must have been the potion she'd swallowed earlier that was causing her to act so much like a crazed hyena.

I considered. I didn't know of any potion or spell that could help me get her back. If I had paid a bit more attention to my witchery studies previously, I might have had an idea, but nothing was coming into my brain right then. Zero.

Zip!

I felt around the walls. Astonishingly, I couldn't feel *anything*! I walked over to one wall, expecting to break out easily, but of course, as usual, I could only hurt myself.

Jenny stared at me, appearing to be intrigued and slightly amused as I bumped myself (hey, you would be too, if you witnessed a maniac bumping against something that wasn't there), looking dizzy, disoriented, and interested, all at once. If I didn't get her out of this state of affairs IMMEDIATELY, I was going to faint! I was going to collapse right on the spot!

So I did the first immature thing that I could think of: I conjured up a bucket of water and poured every last drop of the contents over her head.

Jenny gave a bloodcurdling scream.

This last action reversed the effect that the potion had on her, and she began to show symptoms of acute ADHD (Attention Deficit Hyperactivity Disorder) for a period of time. As I watched her run around the little "prison firewall," I began to wonder whether or not I should send her off to a mental hospital once we got out of this place—I mean, *if* we ever got out of this place.

After a moment or two of this unsettling hyperactivity, she looked at me for a minute with a lost expression. Then her eyes readjusted and she refocused on my face. I decided I had better explain to her why she was in this appalling state.

"Jenny, I'm sorry. I have no idea what happened, except that you swallowed a few drops of this potion, and then you started acting like—"

"A hobo from the seventeenth—no, twentieth century BC," Jenny offered, giggling.

"With a mutilated porcupine," I added. Velvet whimpered, as if she knew she was being made fun of. "Don't worry," I whispered into her fuzzy, droopy little ear. "We don't mean it at all."

"So anyway," I said, getting back to the point. "We're locked inside this firewall thingy, and as far as I can tell, we can't get out. What should we do? Start acting like you?"

Jenny knocked the walls with her knuckles. She couldn't feel anything, of course, but they turned white anyway. "It's not hollow," she told me. "That means it's gonna be way harder to get out of this place."

"*Yeah, like that info is gonna help improve the situation,*" I mumbled sarcastically.

Jenny gave me one of those looks. "It's not that hard, you know," she said, tossing her hair over her shoulder.

"Then what do we do?!" I cried, getting exasperated.

Jenny tried to look confident, but it wasn't helping matters. "Um, how am I supposed to know?" she demanded. "All I know is that it can't possibly be as hard as they make it out to be. I know those witchy scientist-assistant weirdos have very strong powers, and we can't even get into the vague neighborhood of matching them, but there has to be an alternative. There's a catch here. I just know that there is."

"What do you mean?" I asked.

"It's simple. I told you that the walls aren't hollow, which means there's no escape from that route. But take a look at those video cameras over there. Touch them. Do you feel anything?"

I touched them. They felt like…well…air. Just like the wall did.

"So what about them?" I inquired, perplexed.

"Don't you get it?!" She was obviously much smarter than I was. "They're only textured holograms, just like this wall! The wall is too big and strong for us to destroy, but the cameras aren't. So if we direct both of our magic at the cameras at the same time, we can destroy them! The cameras and the motion sensors also control the strength of the firewall!"

I just stared at her for a minute, almost stunned beyond belief. Then, "Jenny, you're a genius!"

"I know, right!" Jenny agreed, looking smug.

"But wait," I cautioned suddenly. "What type of magic are we directing exactly? Because I don't want to mess this spell up like I've always done before."

Most unfortunately, before I could say anything more, the door opened automatically and a chemist in an electric green lab coat stepped in. He calmly strutted right across the room to our prison cell, not even bothering to walk around the table and chairs, as they too automatically parted in half for him like the Red Sea. Jenny and I huddled together nervously, waiting for what seemed like our executions.

He muttered a spell and threw open the emerging glass door. He didn't say anything. He was way too close for comfort.

He stared at us for a moment, as if making sure his prisoners hadn't escaped, then paraded out of the room with swag. I let out a whopper-size breath. Our plan to go through the building undetected had backfired completely, but there was still some hope left for us.

Jenny whispered into my ear after he had left the room, almost knocking off my dangly crystal earrings. "Direct your bursts of magical force to the cameras and motion sensors to disable them. Just use regular bursts of magic...y'know, the kind that's just meant to overwhelm inanimate objects. We have to do it at the exact same time for it to be strong enough to get us out of here," she instructed.

"Mm-hmm...overwhelm *inanimate* objects...whatever that means..." I replied absent-mindedly, glaring intently at the cameras and putting all my magic into my eyes. My eyes got this red-hot, fiery sensation, and it felt like they were burning. I had no opportunity to glance over even briefly at Jenny. If I'd actually had the opportunity, I would have noticed that she was performing the spell with a whole lot less effort than it was taking me.

After about sixty seconds of this heated torture (for me), we shot through the firewall and ended up free to go in the conference room.

There was just *one…minor…problem.*

The whole place was beeping.

Beeping, screeching, and absolutely *buzzing* with activity.

I ran out of the room to find what seemed to be hundreds of random people in lab coats coming after me. Jenny shot temporary paralyzing spells at a few of them, and they froze in mid-dash. I ducked under some conference chairs in the next room while the scientist people were distracted.

I heard them saying something to each other. Apparently, they were going to split up and search for us. How unfortunate! I looked frantically for some other way out of the room but could find none. This situation became far worse when I found four scientists blocking the doorway. And where was Jenny?

I screamed.

"JENNIFER! WHERE ARE YOU?!"

The wall crumbled to dust behind me. Jenny, looking utterly exhausted, pulled me through the pile of rubble. It reconstructed itself automatically. I stared at her. Was it even possible for someone her age to know such advanced magic?

In the next room, there were eight or nine scary-looking wizards guarding the room. They started to move toward us. I remembered a curse I'd read about in one of those immensely boring witchcraft textbooks. And it didn't involve a bunch of random chanting.

"*FIRE RING!*" I shouted.

Bluish flames erupted around Jenny and me. The wizards stepped back.

"*ICE TRANSFORMATION!*" one of them yelled.

The flames turned cold. They had stopped simmering.

As the scientist people advanced toward us, Jenny shrank the flames. I managed to step over them just as one of the wizards planted himself in front of me.

Well. Just as I thought we had escaped, this had to happen.

He raised his hand in front of his pale, ghostly face and tried to perform a spell that would probably kill me just as I noticed the table behind us. Vials of potion? Escape? There was a connection. I felt strangely calm and collected.

I had no idea what the potions on that table would do, but I seized one anyway and smashed the test tube over the wizard's head.

His eyes glazed over, and he fell to the ground in a heap. Not dead, I assumed, just knocked out. Anyway, that took care of him.

My eyes wandered over the rest of the chaotic scene. Most of the scientists had disappeared, presumably to think up some better means of recapturing us. Jenny was shouting shield incantations at the guy in front of her as he resorted to physical fighting. Her silky blond hair was literally on fire, with flames shooting off from the ends. It looked harmless, so I didn't do anything about it. Shattered glass and steaming, bubbling potions were scattered all over the tiled floor.

A different guy, I realized, was also sneaking up behind her. I was standing alone in the middle of the floor with no one cornering me, and I tried to think up a way to help her. The potions, it seemed, were my only choice.

I grabbed one of the last unbroken containers and flung it at the person Jenny was fighting. Unfortunately, I hadn't thought much about my aim. Instead of hitting the wizard, it hit *her*!

Uh-oh, I thought; now I was thoroughly doomed. Jenny had immediately turned into a squawking parrot, and there was nothing that I could do about it. Or was there?

There simply had to be a way. I quickly conjured up a Sense-Depriving Draught (how did I do that?!) and threw it—carefully—at the scientist in front of me. It hit him full in the face. Nice! He began to babble uncontrollably. I sighed with relief before I realized that something was happening to me. I must have been enchanted by someone.

My hair, clothes, body, and face, were all changing colors. I was sleepy…oh so sleepy. I wanted to sink down in a field of pansies and just faint. I wanted to go into a deep sleep and never wake up. I wanted to…

Suddenly, I felt like I was being pulled through a long tunnel. There was a light at the end of it. It was a nice light, radiating warmth and happiness. It reminded me of Santa, who, of course, existed. Mickey Mouse was dashing toward me, reciting nursery rhymes. I felt myself lunging into the wonderful world of Mother Goose and her baby—what were they—baby ducklings? Curious George was so interesting. I was a sleeping child—

"ZARA, WOULD YOU PLEASE WAKE UP THIS INSTANT!" I heard someone hissing in my ear.

My eyes slowly opened. Jenny was standing over me, a human Jenny, not a parrot.

"What—how...Am I dreaming?" I babbled most illogically. "And where did Mickey Mouse go?!"

"Shut up or they'll hear us," she snarled through gritted teeth. "I'll explain this later. All I'm going tell you now is that I've found a dark room. No one else is here..."

Seventeen

Breakthrough

Jenny grabbed my arm and, without even telling me what she was about to do, teleported us rapidly to the outside of the premises. The inhabitants of the lab couldn't get out past the courtyard or the firewall that they had, rather ironically, created by themselves.

I ended up, of course, naturally, sprawling on the ground in an unsightly mess, with my hair whipping around my now makeup-drained face and my dress almost clean ripped through. Jenny did not look like *nearly* such a spectacle. Thinking quickly, she zapped my dress, making it spotless, straightened out my stripy hair, and sprinkled a little make-you-undisoriented sparkle spell over me.

"We're fine," she assured me. "But, moldy cheese, we almost didn't get through that place!"

"I know, right," I grunted. "How are you back to a human again?"

"I spotted one of the last remaining intact potions on the table. Of course, being the total genius I am, I recognized it immediately. It was a potion for reverse incantation."

"Omigosh," I gasped. "So you used it. But is there *any* left? *ANY?*"

"No. Sorry."

I sighed dejectedly. This was the second time I'd gotten so close yet so far from transforming Allie into her chubby, blue-and-neon-pink-haired self again. Well, at least we were one step closer.

"But," she continued, draining my spirits through yet again, "we still have a long way to go. The magic-depriving forest, 'member? A.k.a. the MDF."

"You really seem to adore acronyms, don't you?" I asked.

"Whatevs. Though *you* seem to just loooooove TSHs," she shot back. "And *you're welcome* for me saving your life multiple times."

"Sorry. I mean, thanks," I acquiesced helplessly.

"Anyway, to help in the apparently increasingly complicated process of waking you up, I think that it might make life just *a little bit* easier to show you something impressive before we continue on our journey," she said.

Now, *that* woke me up.

"Technology or magic?" I questioned, though I already knew the answer. Technology, naturally. To us witches, magic is tiresome, not fascinating. Ordinary things are far more exciting.

"Technology," she answered obliviously, busily pressing buttons on her DSX. I watched in amazement as a 3-D textured hologram of a green spinning star was instantaneously generated from the device.

"What's your favorite animal?" she asked.

"A kitten," I replied. "But what exactly do you plan to do with that particular info?"

"Wait and see," she responded.

In a flash of blinding pink, the spinning hologram turned into a textured, frolicking, animated gray kitten.

"Oh my gosh!" I squealed. "It's so cute!"

"Wait. That's not all." Jenny grinned, flipping a remote. "Walk around to the other side—yeah, that's it. Now look at the hologram. What do you see?"

I gasped. When I looked at the hologram at a slightly different angle, the kitten dissolved into sparkles and an animated, touchable hologram of Velvet appeared. "Awwwwww!" I cooed. "It's *beautiful*! But where did you get the animation video clips from? They're so *lifelike*!"

"I didn't need to record them from anywhere, you hobo," she said, rolling her icy blue eyes. "They're QPC generated. Remember, those 'quantum personal computers' that I told you about?"

"Yeah, of course I do. I don't have a short-term memory deficit, you know," I retorted.

"Well, I guess that means you're ready to go," Jenny deadpanned with a blank expression. She slung her purse over her shoulder and held on to it tightly, causing her knuckles to turn a dead-looking white.

"How do we get there?" I inquired.

Jenny looked at her DSX and frowned. She seemed to be mapping out some kind of route. Then she groaned. Loudly, like a malfunctioning piece of equipment stuck in an ancient train engine.

"Moldy cheese with rotten ketchup and Spam, we came out on the wrong side of the building!"

Another abnormally noisy groan escaped, except this time from me. "*Oh dear!* Moldy cheese, this is ludicrous!" I exclaimed.

"I'm really rubbing off on you, aren't I?" Jenny observed, smiling *for once*.

I grunted. "Well, how do we get to the other side? The firewall will block the teleportation anyway, so that's not an option. *Will we really have to go through the building again*?"

"No, we won't. I have an idea. But it has to work," Jenny informed me. "See the firewall over there? Well, I mean, you can't exactly *see* it, or even *feel* it, for that matter, but I'll tell you one thing—there are video cameras and motion sensors *inside* the building, and due to the theory of interconnectivity and everything, since we disabled the cameras *inside*, this firewall will be really easy to break down! So all we have to do is teleport ourselves to the other side. Easy! And since the video cameras' damage is irreparable for at least the next few years because of our powerful combined magic, any well-meaning witch can just teleport themselves to the other side!"

I listened to this whole statement feeling enthralled by it all.

"So teleport us there," I ordered.

A few seconds later, we materialized on the other side of the building, outside of the opposite courtyard. In front of us was what looked like a thick sea of greenery. I looked at it helplessly.

"Why in the world is that witchy HQ guarded like this? An insane chemistry lab, a forest, saber-toothed, hypnotic dragons—it's outrageous!" I declared.

"Who knows?" Jenny responded with a hint of annoyance. "Don't ask idiotic questions that have no answers. The thing is, anyway, even if you're a witch with limited magical skills/powers, like we are, you should be able to get through at least the laboratories. The forest is another story. It surrounds the witchy

HQ on all sides anyway, so it's of no use trying to take shortcuts."

"But our magic goes away in that forest. Shouldn't we, y'know, conjure up more food and stuff to last us through?" I suggested.

"Definitely," she agreed, beginning to do some clapping/stamping thing with her body. She struck at the ground with one of her wedge-heeled, ruffly, fuzzy-ish boots. Immediately, Oreos, lemon-flavored marshmallows, more pizza, and a truckload of candy appeared.

"Cool!" I squealed. "We can eat whatever we want!"

Eighteen

Forest Thunderstorm

The forest, at first glance, was just a huge thicket of greenery. The canopies of trees overhead made the place look deep and dark in broad daylight, though it probably wasn't. I wondered where we would be sleeping for the night. This place looked a whole lot as if it were permanently deprived of any inhabitants.

Jenny was looking at a compass (Amazing! And in this time period too!) as the sky darkened overhead. The cotton candy-colored clouds appeared again, signaling sunset. Rainbow-colored sparkles swam across the clouds and completed the scene, making the sky tinted with lavender.

"We travel straight north," she announced. "Not hard, if the dragons don't intercept us or cast spells on us. But for right now, it's past ten o'clock and already sunset, so I can see that we'd better find a place to sleep!"

"*Already* sunset?" I mimicked mockingly as if it were supposed to be some kind of leg-puller joke.

"Sure. It has something to do with the position of the Earth's orbit shifting or somethin' hard to understand like that because of a mega-sized asteroid knocking into Pluto and upsetting the natural order of the solar system. In fact, scientists predict that in the next forty or so years Neptune will intercept Uranus's orbit and they'll switch places. The collision happened, like, sixty years ago, and you should know that by now. It's history," Jenny chided as if it were the most obvious thing in the whole world.

"Um, in case you've forgotten, I time traveled to get here," I muttered, while rolling out my sleeping bag on a soft, almost *cuddly* piece of moss under a rocky outcrop/cave-like thing.

"Oh, all right," Jenny acquiesced.

✳ ✳ ✳

The next morning brought peppy sunshine and an incessant, light breeze that whistled through everything and brought an end to the perpetual stillness of the night.

I hexed my sleeping bag to fold itself up automatically and then wandered across to Jenny's bag like a forest-roving vagrant. Jenny was still fast asleep, her hair flowing across her face like a cascading waterfall of silk.

I stole over to Jenny's purse, which was hanging down by her elbow, and pulled out a bag of popcorn, realizing that I actually hadn't eaten a single morsel for the whole of the day before. I was absolutely ravenous. I had finished almost the whole gigantic bag (which was miniaturized but automatically resized when we ate: technology), completely forgetting to conserve apparent resources, when Jenny woke up.

"That's enough popcorn eating," she scolded. "At this rate, we'll never get to the witchy HQ if we spend all of our time partying!"

The daytime wasn't very eventful. I questioned Jenny about the dragons and wondered if there were other species here.

"Not that I know of," Jenny said. "Even if there were other species, the dragons would wipe them out anyway. The dragons are definitely the dominant species here."

"How many dragons are there?" I inquired.

"It depends on what part of the forest you're in. Where we're walking through, there's a whole lot of rocky caves, so I'm guessing it's one family per mile, on average."

"Yikes," I muttered.

The forest didn't really change much as we walked through it. There was the thick undergrowth of different kinds of bushes, then the slightly smaller trees all around, then the huge ones, which formed what seemed to be never-ending canopies over the forest and blocked out the light almost completely. The whole place looked and felt really desolate. Jenny informed me that the dragons were, for the most part, mainly active during the day.

They ate almost anything. Any plant, to be exact, however poisonous it was. This was ironically funny, though—the dragons were vegetarian! The forest probably wouldn't provide much of any meat anyway, so I guess they were much better off like that.

That evening, though, it became stiflingly hot. I had the sudden urge to throw off my dress or turn it into something cotton, but I didn't have my magic powers anymore, and anyway this was the only dress that I'd brought for the journey.

Velvet was irritable, hot, sweaty, and altogether in a very bad mood. For the first time, her good behavior wore off totally. She yipped, yapped, tugged at the leash, barked, whimpered, and lost it completely. She drove me absolutely bananas!

After a while, though I had sworn not to lose any of our precious food supply with Velvet's idiotic and time-consuming antics, now I just gave in. She contentedly gobbled down a pack of Oreos and a pizza slice. Ordinarily, it's considered extremely bad to feed your dog processed human food items like that, but Velvet was no ordinary dog, and I figured that she could probably put up with it.

This was right before the gales started. They began as light winds that were merely whistling through the trees, but they soon became winds of several full-force, possibly category three, dangerous hurricanes (OK, I'm being dramatic). I had to hold Velvet in my arms to save the leash from snapping itself in two.

Pretty soon, dazzling, brilliant flashes of lightning began to illuminate the dark night sky, followed by rumbling thunder. They lit up the forest scene with their vivid, intense illumination. Jenny ran around the place frantically looking for somewhere we could take shelter.

Soon, the rain really began to pelt down. Hard. I ducked into a random, rocky cave that Jenny had just found behind an overflowing stream and rapidly flowing miniature waterfall. We felt squished but relieved.

I still don't know how long we waited in that cave. I estimated it to be around six hours, but I could never know for sure. All I know is that I miraculously managed to actually drift off to sleep while the thunderstorm raged outside. I think we spent the night crouching in that cave.

We crawled out from under it at around five the next morning, feeling lethargic and exhausted. I barely noticed the enticing summer scene outside, with flowers blooming and bees buzzing and birds chirping and butterflies whizzing around the flowers and whatnot. Talk about a desert rainstorm!

We ate marshmallows for "breakfast." I wondered what my own mother would think if she knew what was going on right now. Jenny's mom was probably feeling worse. I couldn't help thinking about what was gonna happen to her when she finally got home. But one thing was for sure: it *definitely* wouldn't be pleasant.

Nineteen

The Dragon Cave

The next day was similar, except for the thunderstorm that had taken place on the previous day.

Jenny estimated that we had gone about ten miles so far by the end of the day. Apparently, despite the storm and all of the holdups, we were right on schedule.

Dragons, thankfully, had not intercepted us yet, but with their one-family-per-mile population density, I couldn't help feeling that it was going to be the inevitable. I was still feeling like I was in a ridiculous situation, though. How in the world had I come from messing with spells in my own house and turning my little sister into a bunny to ending up in a dragon-infested forest two hundred plus years in the future? It was outrageous! Blasphemous! Preposterous! Outlandish! Absurd! Bizarre! Nonsensical! Otherworldly! Ludicrous! Fanatical! Extreme! Eccentric! Totally, completely, utterly, starkly, downright, blatantly, absolutely, positively WILD!

That night, we had an unusually difficult time finding ourselves a place to sleep. Usually the forest was punctuated with various types of rocky caves, but this time it seemed to be utterly deprived of them.

Soon enough, though, I found what appeared to be a very large sledge of rock jutting out from some undergrowth. It was, in fact, quite perceptibly in the neighborhood of ten feet tall. I was pleasantly surprised, but a little scared when it came to investigating it.

I called Jenny over, and together we hashed away the briar-covered undergrowth and ended up with horribly unmanicured hands that were, at the end of the violent hashing, positively streaming with blood. I barely had enough time to perceive the pain, though, because of what was inside that cave.

I shook away the remaining bushes and peered inside, hardly able to believe my eyes. Because inside that cave were eight or nine huge, greenish eggs nestled among a bed (or should I say, *nest*) of extremely prickly and altogether most uninviting thorns.

Dragon eggs. Baby dragon eggs.

Again, naturally, of course, as usual, I *almost* squealed, but Jenny managed to clamp a hand over my mouth just in time.

"Rotten ketchup, it's a dragons' nest, all right!" she said. "But their mother or father or whoever who takes care of them will be somewhere around here. It's dangerous. I don't like it. I have a feeling that we'll have to sleep with fire tonight. I'll light a couple of candles and have them flickering around our cave all night to scare away any dragons that venture here immediately."

"But I thought that they *breathe* fire. How can they be afraid of it?" I questioned, confused.

"These are a different species of dragons. Sure, they breathe smoke, but not *fire*. In fact, I don't think any species of dragons breathe fire. It may be just a myth," Jenny explained sweetly. "Just like how every-one thinks mermaids are so gorgeous and beautiful, when actually they're hideous savage *beasts.* I don't recommend you get in the path of one."

"Oh," I sighed, relieved by this new information (the part about the dragons, NOT the mermaids). "When will they hatch?"

Jenny looked surprised suddenly. "Dragons gener-ally hatch during the summer," she enlightened me. "But it's early autumn already. So I'm thinking maybe they'll hatch tonight!"

"*Oh my gosh!*" I squealed. "Can we visit them, like, tomorrow morning?!"

Jenny gave me that look, so I added hastily, "Y'know, when their mom or whoever isn't around?"

"For heaven's sake, they're *dragons*, not stuffed toys, Zoey! You can't just go and play with them whenever you want to, whether or not their mother is home or foraging for something to eat! They're dangerous!" Jenny sounded like my mom when she's starting off a mind-boggling lecture.

✳ ✳ ✳

We finally found a suitable place to sleep. Most unfortunately, it was out in the open air and near the dragon cave, but it was obscured by overhanging foli-age, so we figured that it would be OK. Jenny took out a couple of KwikLite matches, four or five candles, and the match box. I was, and still am, terrified of fire, so I, like the dragons, resolved not to go anywhere near the flames.

Just as Jenny was preparing to light the first can-dle, though, a sudden gust of wind whipped the flame over from the candle to her bare hand. She let out a small scream and made me pour freezing cold water over her fingers in order to keep them from burning. They were already scarred.

And that was the end of *that* idea. As much as the flames could have helped us, Jenny would not handle them again. In all honesty with myself, I couldn't blame her. I mean, how many people can actually play around with fire without feeling jittery?

I felt increasingly restless that night. We had left our purses and food outside of the cave so that if the dragons smelled it and came to get it, then they wouldn't discover us as well—a terribly risky and precarious precaution, so to speak.

I guess that I must have eventually fallen asleep because the next thing I knew, I was sitting up, shaking, and listening in terror as a loud hissing sound came from right outside of our hiding place. I didn't have to think or reason; I already knew what that noise was: *the dragons.*

They had discovered our food supply.

I sat stiller than a stone statue (they erode over long periods of time, don't they?) while the hideous creatures raided our purses. I could hear the rip of dragon claws against my purse's delicate Coach fashion fabric, and it wasn't pretty: much like that of a zombie's superlong nails scratching against sandpapered chalkboard. A blatantly terrible, horrible, petrifying, horrifying, terrifying, awful, dreadful, appalling, horrendous, severely frightful, nasty, atrocious, ghastly, hideous, repulsive, sickening, disheartening, vile, unpleasant, upsetting, horrific, demoralizing sound. Well, actually, on second thought, maybe it wasn't *that* bad. But it was bad enough to make me pretty dizzy.

After what seemed like a couple of years…perhaps a millennium…perhaps a few hundred eternities of tension, the scratching sounds stopped. I waited for a minute or two and then cautiously ventured to take a peek through the sheet of moss that hid our cave from plain sight. No one, or rather, *no dragon*, was there. And sure enough, our purses were gone as well. Maybe not completely gone, but totally ripped to unprepossessing, ghastly shreds of beautiful fabric. Oh, the poor purses! I seriously considered, for a minute, having a funeral for the poor, wretched inanimate objects. But then I thought better of it; though it *was* really distressing to witness the damage that the dragons had done to the pieces of innocent fabric. I found myself sniffling…or *NOT!* The drama had been passed on to slightly more pressing issues, such as… where were we going to get more food from? Could we ever get it back? How could we?

I rolled over and hoped to get some sleep. Such irrelevant matters could wait to be decided until morning. Only then did I notice that I hadn't been the only one who was disturbed by the ruckus. Jenny was sitting bolt upright, staring at me, and her face looked as if she really ought to be in the ICU unit in the hospital (I already told you about those, so I sincerely hope that you don't have short-term memory loss). Her blond hair looked a great deal as if it had just been stampeded on by an oversized pack of wild, bull-horned cattle…Or maybe a small mammal made a nest in there, eloped with its to-be husband to get married, and left the nest to stay messed up for the remainder of its most horribly pointless and most terribly worthless life. I almost laughed out loud. And please use your common sense and take note of the terribly obvious fact that I said *almost*, as in the meaning of *very nearly*.

"W-what just happened?" Apparently the force of the insistent stampeding had given Jenny a concussion. "Did the dragons take our food? What will we do? Where will we get more? What if the babies hatched? How will we search the nest? Will we starve? Will we die? Oh no! I just altogether can't believe that this is happening! We're dead! We're *DOOMED*!"

I giggled. "Listen, you idiot! They did take our food, but I somehow doubt that the dragon babies have hatched yet, so all that we have to do is to stalk the dragon mother, wait for our chance, and take the food to safety. See? Easy! Except for the dragon-mom-stalking part," I added quickly.

"Yeah! That sounds, like, super easy! In fact, it may even be *fun*! Perhaps it may even help us out in those particular *skillz* areas if we want to be witchy detectives when we grow up!" Jenny shouted out with a horribly blunt hint of sarcasm.

I grunted. "We'll talk it over in the mornin', Jenny," I droned in an unnecessarily and exceedingly bored monotone voice. "No time now. I wanna get some *sleep*!"

Twenty

Ghastly Dragon Encounter

As previously expected, we had nothing for "breakfast" the next morning, not even candy. I felt miserable and irritable.

"So, what will we do about this outrageously ridiculous situation?" I questioned Jenny.

"We need to track the mother in order to see when she usually leaves the nest," Jenny responded. "Then, assuming that the baby dragons haven't hatched, we'll go in and get the food."

"But what if they *have* hatched?" I insisted.

"We'll cross that bridge when we come to it," Jenny lectured.

I rolled my eyes. "What's our first move? Should we go to the cave? Because I haven't even had breakfast yet, and I'll let you know that I'm really *hungry*," I complained.

"Sure you are. So am I. Luckily, the dragon species that live in this particular forest haven't got very good hearing, smell, vision, or other sharp senses, so it should be relatively easy to wait outside the cave for the dragon mother to emerge. She's particularly active around this time of day…or, as we saw yester-day, around dusk," Jenny instructed confidently.

I groaned. "Jenny, I'm most terribly sorry about interrupting your endless, perpetual, meaningless, useless, and highly consistent lecturing, but I simply *can't* go on with my life without knowing…How do you know so much about the forest?"

"It's simple. Pretty much every single witch does…around *here*. It's in our witchery studies," she answered.

"Well, what are we waiting for?" I demanded. "We should be leaving to go to the cave!"

"What are *you* waiting for, delaying us like this with your annoying questions?!" Jenny retorted rudely. "Sorry. But we've gotta go right now. Wait…*Where* was the dragon cave again?"

"Um," I said.

And yes, of course, naturally, we wound up getting completely, utterly lost in the depths of the dragon forest. Jenny took out her compass since she couldn't use her DSX; there was no Wi-Fi or whatever it's called in this era here in the forest. We were travel-ing straight north like we were supposed to still, but we'd have to retrace our steps. I was a little peeved at Jenny, though, to be honest. She was *supposed* to be my guide, wasn't she…?

Eventually, though, we found the ten-foot-tall rocky cave. A whole lot of unwelcome heat seemed to be emanating from it. I drew back suddenly, startled by the intense, sweltering, stuffy heat.

"How do we get into there? What do we do?" I whispered frantically to Jenny.

"It's simple. We wait," she replied, sounding far too calm and collected for the present state of affairs near the cave.

And we waited. We waited, hidden under some scratchy, cherry-blooming, dragon-laurel bushes near the cave. It was not at all fun, by any means. Waiting just happens to be one of the worst ways to squander precious time. I did not enjoy it. I did not enjoy it at all.

Most unfortunately, though, as usual, the incredibly complicated process of waiting began to make me feel jittery. I whispered to Jenny again, even more frantically than before.

"Jenny! What the heck are we waiting soooooo loooooong out here for?! The dragon mother simply *must* have gone by now!" I thundered impatiently.

"Relax. She'll be in there somewhere," Jenny answered, her icy blue eyes on the cave.

And right on cue, as we watched, a smoke-breathing, horribly scaly, wickedly grinning, tail-swishing, small-yellow-eyes-blazing, bright-green-wings-fluttering, and thoroughly-creeping-me-out creature ambled out of the cave entrance. I almost died at the sight. It was epically horrendous.

As the creature sniffed at the air, sending choking, huge spires of smoke out from its gruesome nostrils, it lumbered away from the cave. I realized that I'd been holding my breath, and I let it out heavily. Rather unsurprisingly, I had never seen a dragon before, let alone one that wasn't a toy (discovering something that *[I thought]* doesn't exist used to be a most enthralling and fulfilling experience). For a fleeting moment, I sort of wanted to see a vampire.

Once that hideous creature was thoroughly out of sight, we clambered into the cave. Most unfortunately for me, the dragon eggs hadn't hatched yet. The popcorn, pizza, candy, marshmallows, etc., were nowhere to be seen. I was piqued and irritated. And I didn't at all see why dragons should enjoy human delicacies anyhow.

Just when we were about to make a thorough hunt through the cave, I heard a crinkling, cracking sound behind me. My blood pressure skyrocketed. One of the dragons had hatched, and I was absolutely ecstatic, overjoyed, in seventh heaven, swimming in euphoria, enraptured, elated, delighted, thrilled, delirious, excited, captivated, or however you care to put it. But it was only one egg. I had taken it for granted that they would all hatch together.

The baby dragon was, aside from its tiny smoke-breathing nostrils, pretty cute—not utterly adorable, but somewhere within the margin of slightly cute and downright adorable I guess. I wanted to take the little thing home, but as you know, I've told you about the zoo that I have already…and I'm not exactly sure that my mom would want a potentially ten-foot-long, smoke-breathing, and horribly scaly dragon in the house along with everything else. Plus, it might eat both our pantry *and* our refrigerator clean out of food. Just an observation!

Jenny was completely engulfed in the horribly pointless and most meaningless activity of shooting fiery daggers out of her eyes at me while I petted the dragon. It actually seemed to like me! I guess that it's just a simple matter of getting to know the dragons better, and then they'll like you (I was not exactly in a fully conscious and intelligent state at that *particular* moment in time). Neither of us noticed the scaly, smoke-expelling creature outside of the cave but awfully near us. Velvet, as well, was playing with the baby dragon. Rather surprisingly, Jenny also seemed to like the baby.

"I love it! It really *is* cute, after all." Jenny giggled while stroking the dragon. "I thought it would be vicious, but it's not!" Then, suddenly, she gave an ear-piercing, blood-curdling, high-decibel-level scream. "Unlike its mother! YIKES!"

We dashed out of the cave and back to our quarters while the full-grown dragon got back to her babies. I still had mine—the hatched one, I mean—in my hand. Velvet was busy nudging it with her nose.

"What, exactly, are we planning to do with this thing?!" I panted, once we had gotten back to our own cave.

"*You're* the one who brought it in," Jenny pointed out accusingly.

"How was I supposed to know that the evil, vicious beast was going to get back so soon?" I wailed.

"Too bad! But we have to return it! There is absolutely no way under the witchy continuum that I am going to be caught bringing a *dragon* into the HQ premises! They'll think that we've gone completely crazy, which *you* may have anyhow, but *I* most definitely have *not*, and *I* don't want to make that kind of an outrageously horrendous first impression! What kind of dummy do you take me for?" she hollered uncontrollably.

"A mentally unhinged, crazy, eccentric, outlandish FANATIC who is most deficient in common sense and who has multiple multifaceted self-esteem issues!" I screeched nonsensically. "And what's more, may I ask, just WHO do YOU take ME for?! YOURSELF?!" I shrieked back at her, sounding like a highly mentally imbalanced lunatic myself.

You can probably quite easily imagine how each of us was feeling as if we were extremely senseless outlaws who must have somehow escaped the asylum and, most importantly, the mentally imbalanced and senile crazies ward, though I had absolutely no idea how or why that it was so. I thought that maybe the dragons had somehow, inexplicably, enchanted us...?

Anyway, after all of that outlandish ranting, we finally...*whew!*...got back to our senses, and we held a council of war.

"Let's get back to the dragon cave," I suggested. "Once the mother goes out again, I mean. I'm starving, and we need food. We're not going to starve, since the forest's exit can't be more than a couple of miles away, but I need food. Even *moldy cheese* would work..."

"My curses aren't food, Zoey, though currently I wish they were. I'm exhausted, but there's only one option. We have to go back to that nest. Maybe if we offer the dragon mother her baby, she'll take it as a peace offering...?" Jenny muttered, still looking slightly bewildered.

Twenty One

Stone Statue

By the time we had ventured back to the dragon cave, the dragon mother had gone out again to forage for food even though she obviously already had some...*ours.*

This time, though, neither of us waited for anybody, or, in more explicit terms, any *dragon.* We just ran into the cave and returned the baby dragon to its nest, where the other baby dragons had evidently just hatched, since they were crawling out of their abnormally large, green, blob-like eggs. Jenny seemed to be under some kind of spell by the dragon babies.

Suddenly, she let go of the dragon that she was assiduously stroking and turned to me. "I don't think that the dragons are originally from here," she murmured in an enchanted voice.

"What do you mean, *not from here*?" I asked.

"What I mean is, even though they're babies, they would be vicious if they were an evolving species from here," she answered.

I stroked and petted one of the lizard-like things with white wings and suddenly understood what she meant. "They don't want to be here any more than we do," I said softly.

"Exactly! And I bet that they're from a different time period," Jenny expounded excitedly but angrily. "Someone brought them here!"

I considered this. "I bet it was that stupid, evil, witchy scientist from the chemistry laboratory who did it!" I exclaimed. "Let's bring one of them to the witchy HQ to show the witches there so that they can transport them back to wherever they belong! This is so awesome!"

"Don't jump to conclusions," Jenny scolded me. "But we are definitely going to show this to them. Bring the dragon baby that you already made friends with, Zoey. It will be a whole lot more cooperative than the other ones, I think."

"But the first priority is the food. I can't find it!" I hollered suddenly.

"HUNT AROUND!" she barked like a boys' football team coach on steroids. On second thought, I think she sounded like that most of the time.

We looked in every little nook and cranny inside of that cave, but it didn't yield any results. I was most disappointed.

Jenny fished around her sweater and found her compass (ah...the more primitive means of finding your way!). She frowned and then gasped. "We've come a whole lot farther than we previously thought. Moldy cheese, this is so awesome! Only one mile and a half left!" she squealed.

I laughed. "We'll get there today then if we keep moving. But how can you tell distance on your compass?" I questioned, elated and incredulous.

"Oh, just some special what-do-you-call-it features this-and-that. You don't need DSX signals for them," she replied happily. "I just forgot about them for a while in my panic, that's all."

"Of course you did," I responded wryly.

"Like you'd be any better," Jenny muttered sardonically under her breath.

✳ ✳ ✳

We walked away from the dragon cave as fast as we could. We figured that we wouldn't really have to worry now that we knew they were not supposed to be in this forest and were terribly miserable, but "throwing away precautions is not going to help," Jenny chided. I gave her a strange look.

On the way back down, I kept on thinking about something that Jenny had said…something about the dragons being…hypnotic?! I definitely doubted that. I mean, what would they even do to us…enchant us? Somehow, I had my doubts about that.

"Hey, Jenny!" I called. "You said that they were, like, hypnotic or something. But they can't be. I mean, we've been around them for like forever now, but they haven't done anything to me!"

"Yet," she put in.

I frowned. "Jenny, are you attempting to imply that it hates me so much, it's going to want to kill me or something?!" I demanded, annoyed.

"I didn't say that."

"You implied it."

"I did not."

"You did."

"No."

"YES!" I shouted, tired of our never-ending arguments.

"But anyway," I continued, "just to see if this poor little creature wants to kill me or not, why don't I look into its eyes?"

"NO! DON'T DO THAT!" Jenny screamed, but it was too late.

I didn't know exactly what happened to me, but I knew that it was going to be bad. I couldn't feel anything, not even myself...My arms and legs were paralyzed. I tried to open my mouth, but I couldn't talk. Everything was covered by a dark and menacing sheet of blackness. And I could've sworn that I heard the baby dragon give a small, regretful whimper, as if it were sorry for what it had done. I wasn't angry with *it*, though; I was angry with myself...If a dragon was hypnotic and you looked into its glistening eyes, then it was inevitable that you were going to become enchanted. Because that poor little baby dragon simply couldn't *help* being hypnotic, could it? I almost felt sorry for it in my current state.

Twenty Two

Out of That Annoying Forest

Jenny's Point of View

Zoey just acts so stupid sometimes. Right now I want to catch her by her hair-dye-covered French braid and yank her into a pot of steaming hot soup made by Chef Piscatti, that "circularly gifted"—oh fine, fat—chef in the famous old-time kids cartoon... What did my history teacher call it...Gurious Ceorge? It doesn't matter anyway. Don't you think I have better things to do in class than listen to my history professor?

But it's not going to be any good to sulk right now, because a) I—we—don't have any food and b) WE JUST NEED TO GET OUT OF HERE!

As you can very well imagine, I am utterly freaked out! I can definitely reach the end of the forest if I manage to go straight north or whatever direction it is and not get lost, but wait...where is Zoey's pet whatever-it-is? Where did it go? I think she called it a flying puppy, although I still think it looks more like a deformed mongoose from the seventeenth century BC to me more than anything else...

Argh, I'll have to retrace my footsteps. And as much as I hate Zoey for letting that otherwise harmless baby dragon enchant her, I can't let that animal be ripped to bits by dragons. Getting dragged out of the Cretaceous period and being brought here has probably made those dragons go insane…

I think I should leave some kind of trail. But what can I use? There are only two directions that I can go, north or south. One will get me back home, and the other will get me to the witchy headquarters or whatever that secret organization of wizardry is. Nah, no trail, it's too easy. If I go east or west, I will just end up somewhere random in this forest, which is a bad idea, but I'm just too tired and I don't want to make the effort. Way to be lazy!

I think I can hear something. Yeah, barking. Babyish barking. It's coming from somewhere over there… YIKES! SQUEE! Whatever that means.

Is it just me, or is that DOG covered in VINES?! She's tied up! That dragon must have magical destructive powers or something (and I keep having to remind myself that she probably does!). It's Wittlebur, that magical sticky plant. I think I'll take down a branch and prod it off.

Yes, it's working. I mean, NO! The Wittlebur is attacking ME now! Thank goodness Velvet is loose so she can distract any other dragons; I don't think they'll hurt her. I was right…The dragon is coming along now. I'm just liking these dragons less and less.

Oh NO! The vines are covering my mouth! I can't even shout out to her anymore! OK, I need to calm down and—calmly—go over the facts. I can't remember if Zoey ever told me the origin of Velvet. (I should seriously have listened to her better, come to think of it. I half can't recall what I even came here for.) I think I'll consider my options. What if Velvet is MAGIC? What if

she's a witch-puppy-hedgehog or something? Tele…
tele…what is it…teleportation, no. TELEPATHIC.
That's it! What if she's actually telepathic and will do
what I tell her to in my brain? Uh-oh, my brain cells
must be dying due to overexertion and lack of food, if
I ever even had a brain. Even for a witch puppy, I don't
think anyone can be telepathic. So that idea is pretty
much ruled out.

I suddenly jerk my head up and notice something
that's been there all along: trees. I have a stroke of
inspiration and frantically try to pull my hands free
of the vines. It doesn't work, so I perform a nonver-
bal severing spell with my mind to push the vines
away from my mouth. I instruct Velvet to pull down
a branch. Understanding what I want her to do, she
gets up on her hind legs (wow), tears the branch away
(double wow), and uses it to saw through the vines,
which are now almost choking me…all with her mouth!
Impressive!

It worked! I seriously need to ask Zoey where she
got such a cool…oh fine, puppy from.

Part B

Twenty Three

Awake Again

I awoke dazed. I couldn't seem to remember anything. Recollection was far beyond impossible. Who was the girl sitting next to me on the grass, and why was the daylight so blinding?! We were sitting in front of what looked like a futuristic building with a bunch of trees behind it.

The girl looked most annoyed to realize that I actually existed. She twirled a lock of blond hair in her hand and asked contemptuously, "Do you know what a stupid thing you just did, Zoey? That dragon turned you into *stone*!"

I futilely attempted contemplating the situation, but it was of no use. Dozens of questions were swarming my mind. Who was this girl? Who was Zoey, who had evidently been turned into stone? Why the heck was a large lizard-like thing with wings staring at me so fondly...compassionately, even? Where was I? *Who was I?!* What was this castle-wall thingy in front of me, and why in the world was it there? Why did this girl have some high-tech device in her hand? Was I in the future...whoever I was?

"Zoey, don't tell me that you can't remember any-thing! You are a witch, remember? And you turned your sister into…ummmmmm…was it a bunny?"

"What is a witch?" I murmured inarticulately.

Jenny sighed and shot me an overly disbelieving look. "Go up to that wall."

I did as I was told. Even though I didn't exactly know who Jenny was at that particular moment in time, there was something in her voice that made me listen to her.

"Envision a pink, purple, and sparkly gigantic flower…You're pretty girly, so that should suit you."

I envisioned a pink, purple, sparkly, and girly flower.

"Clap your hands together three times."

I clapped my hands together three times.

"Stomp your feet, um, six times."

I stomped my feet six times.

"Open your eyes. What do you see?"

I opened my eyes and stared in utter amazement. Instead of the wall, there was merely a pink, purple, sparkly, girly, and relatively large hibiscus flower, look-ing as if it were straight out of a princess fairytale thing. I shook my head.

"You're kidding, right? There is no way in this whole unfamiliar world that I am a witch…whatever that is!" I cried. "This whole thing was set up! This is one big joke!"

"No, it's not," she replied calmly. "But apparently it seems like we really *do* need to give you a refresher!"

And before I had even a vague idea/grasp of what was happening, Jenny was swiftly conjuring up a gazillion-liter bucket of iced green tea and dump-ing it over my hair. I gasped and spluttered and looked at her in malevolence (a.k.a. the opposite of munificence, if that makes it any easier to understand, which it probably doesn't).

She laughed maliciously. "You did that to me, remember?"

I looked at her incredulously, my memories flooding back in numerous bits and pieces. Allie…bunny…time travel…Velvet…crazy witchy old lady who just *happened* to be nice…hidden book…more time travel…evil scientist…forest…dragon…oh yeah, *baby* dragon! So Jenny had escaped! The dragon had, *most* unwillingly (or so I hoped), enchanted me and turned me into stone! So *that* was what this hullaballoo was all about!

I shook my head. I couldn't believe it. This was outrageous! Ridiculous! Blasphemous! But wait…oh yeah…I went through *that* list of adjectives already, several times so far.

"So what are we waiting for? Do we enter the witchy HQ right now?" I asked, exasperated.

"Sure, whatevs."

I trudged over to the beautiful flower, picked it, silently whistled a never-dry-out eternal preservation spell onto it, and then stepped easily into the court-yard. There was absolutely nothing that kept me from entering, not a firewall or a high-tech wall, *or* a regular wall, or any kind of a wall, for that matter. But wait…There would be security systems, no doubt.

The door was stout and wooden. It looked really out of place here in this high-tech world, and I was sure that it was meant to look like a cathedral or old-time castle. The door, however, was equipped with what looked like a fingerprinting system, a voice-recognition box, video cameras, touch-screen LED devices, and a whole lot of other stuff that I couldn't figure out.

I stared at it hopelessly. No wonder Goldilocks had used the unlocked door to her advantage!

Jenny followed me to the doorway. She whistled something softly with barely parted lips and sprayed some kind of strawberry ice potion that she had just conjured up out of thin air onto the door, and it flew open. I was so impressed! She must have had really strong powers for that door, with its endless security devices, to respond to her!

We stepped into the front hall. It was nothing like I had imagined it would be. The inside looked extremely different from the outside, not at all like a cathedral, but more like the glossy, glassy-modern buildings that I'd seen earlier. Nobody seemed to be around.

The air seemed to be overflowing with magic; the air had an electric thrum to it. The endless wooden shelves covered the walls completely from ground to ceiling, with hundreds of musty, dusty, fusty, and weathered old books crowding them. I choked back a sneeze. They seemed to be emanating some kind of glittering sparkles, which flew through the air around them in attractive swirls.

There was a small room looking off the front hall, with walls made of glass and a crystal table. But this wasn't just any crystal table; the table itself and all of the stuff on it was magical. Dancing thumbtacks jumped around the table and disguised witchery volumes swayed dangerously in midair. It was most perplexing.

There was a winding staircase leading upward and nothing much else to see. Calling Jenny, I dashed up the stairs.

Most unfortunately for all involved, I hadn't even begun to anticipate what could happen to me while attempting to run up a magical staircase. Consequently, I experienced a most devastating and psychologically traumatic accident. The top half of the staircase turned into *pineapple juice*!

While the unmistakable configuration of the staircase remained, blocks of jello-like pineapple juice still could not possibly support my weight. I tumbled down the staircase and hit my head—*hard*—on the bottom step. I think I must have passed out then, but I still don't really know.

Jenny was looking down at me most disapprovingly around the time that I *think* I woke up. There seemed to be a huge bump on the back of my head, but as I have quite the reputation for imagining things, I doubt that it actually existed. I couldn't speak.

"What *is* going on here?" a tiny and extremely mortified female voice that I knew couldn't be Jenny's suddenly cried.

Twenty Four

A Silly Fairy Thing?!

I looked up wearily. Whizzing around my head, there seemed to be some kind of a miniature silly fairy-like thing, about the size of my open hand. I was tempted to make a grab at it like some kind of a wild, most uncivilized *PHANTOM*; I resisted, even though I knew that I must be hallucinating. It was as simple as that. Fairies did not exist. They were simply young children's silly fairy-thing tale material.

Still, the whizzing noise wasn't stopping, and it became louder and louder. I rubbed my eyes and smoothed out my hair in order to make myself look slightly more presentable, even though I had absolutely no idea of who or what I was presenting myself to. I frowned instinctively.

The tiny female voice began to talk again in its most aggravating and annoying high pitch. I wanted to swat at whoever the voice belonged to.

Eventually, though, I looked up. What I saw was nothing short of a Hollywood sensational. Jenny was standing there, staring, stuttering, looking like she'd just seen a...*Oh, why do we have to go through this word YET AGAIN?*...um...*GHOUL!*

I've never, rather ironically, believed in believing in the unseen even though I use magic (hey! Surprise, surprise! I'm a witch!), and this silly fairy-thing creature was most overwhelming. I just about passed out on the spot—*again*—but thankfully, this time, I managed to overcome it.

The creature was slim and had on a silver, shimmery, way-too-short dress with silver, shimmery, I'd-never-thought-I'd-say-this-but-way-too-sparkly flats and a white pearl necklace; it had soft, silky, lavender, waist-length, wavy hair, with matching deep berry-colored eyes and silver eye makeup. I didn't want to grab her anymore. If she was a silly fairy thing, then I was glad that I had just seen one. As long as I wasn't either dreaming or hallucinating, that was.

"Who are you, where did you come from, how did you get here, and what are you doing here? Are you a witch?" she demanded, looking straight at me.

I gulped. That sure was a whole lot of questions!

"Um, I need help in reversing my sister's enchantment," I managed to squeak out. I felt extremely uncomfortable. Because if there was one thing that I didn't want to become intimidated by, then it was most definitely a *silly fairy thing.*

"Then come with me," she said, her voice lighter and slightly apologetic this time. "Sorry about the staircase. It tends to do that sometimes, as do many other things here. Have you seen the dining table with the mischievous chairs that enjoy turning into whipped cream or shaving cream the moment that you sit on them? It's most annoying, and it makes it quite impossible to have our meals in peace," she rambled.

"Um, are you a *silly fairy thing*?" I asked, trying not to make my voice sound panicked.

"Of course I am, although I must say that I would prefer a more respectable title," she answered, giving me a strange look as she led Jenny and me up the staircase, keeping a very close eye on it this time. "Haven't you seen fairies before? I'm a snowflake fairy. There are lots of fairies here…like, tons of them. You'll see them around. There are violet fairies and autumn fairies and raindrop fairies and plant fairies and coral fairies and jewel fairies and—"

"OK, OK," I interrupted, afraid that she'd try to list all of them in the time that I was there with her. "But what do fairies do here? I mean, I know that they can perform magic, but—"

"Fairies are witches, and witches are fairies," she replied calmly, and with an air of superior knowledge. "You are a fairy as well, but you just need to activate—"

"I am not a silly fairy thing—"

"But you *are* one—"

"But I don't have wings—"

"But I was just saying, you need to activate—"

I began to think that this so-called *silly fairy thing* belonged more in an asylum than anywhere else.

"You are one stupid sprite fairy," Jenny said with conviction. "And I read somewhere that sprites were *talented.*"

"Really? I'm surprised that you read at all," I murmured.

"As I was saying, you need to activate a spell potion that will bring it out. Some witches are born as fairies, and some witches are born as humans. You can easily switch between the two if you know how," the ridiculous fairy thing continued, ignoring Jenny.

"Um, what's your name?" I asked, trying to change the subject.

"My name is Brassica Oleracea Cucumis," she said proudly.

"Oh, great," Jenny muttered. "Why did you have to ask?"

"Do all eccentric witches and fairies have such names?" I asked in annoyance.

"No, my name is unique. It means *Broccoli Cucumber* in English. That's my original Latin name."

OK, *now* I was beginning to seriously wonder whether or not we had come to the right place. I hadn't exactly been sure what to expect when I got here, but mentally unhinged *fairies* who were named after *vegetables* certainly weren't on my list.

After the spiral staircase, we went through hundreds of thousands of corridors full of books (or so it seemed). Right from the floor to the ceiling, books were shelved endlessly. Their spines were all plain pastel colors, dusty, and looked very boring. I didn't bother to read what the spines said. I just needed to get the potion and then be out of there.

Eventually, though, I became curious enough to stop and pull off a book from one of the shelves. I coughed as I looked at the cover. *A Midsummer Night's Dream*, by Shakespeare. How boring! I opened it to the first page, which was the title page, and it had shimmery gold lettering on it. Since the title page told me nothing, I calmly turned to the next one…but most unfortunately, before I actually had the chance to read anything, I felt something cold, runny, and slimy slithering down my wrists.

Instinctively, I screamed.

My screaming echoed off of the walls in that narrow corridor and was magnified gazillions of times (or so it seemed).

"*WHAT THE HECK* IS *THIS THING?*" I hollered, unnerved by the sight and stench of the putrid substance. It was horribly green, horribly snot-appearing, horribly SLIMY, and horribly freaky.

The silly fairy thing, or whatever it was, laughed. "Oh, *that*," she giggled as if it were the most normal thing on the face of the entire universe for a book to suddenly turn into hideous green goop without incantations or warnings from anyone. "It happens sometimes. Goodness knows what that substance is—the books can turn into different things, generally, but we've tested it in a laboratory and it isn't radioactive."

"*Oh, that's* such *a comforting thing to hear,*" I grumbled cynically. Having a book turn into goop was *not* a very good introduction to the witchy HQ.

I thankfully reshelved the book as it morphed back into its original configuration.

"This is the last corridor!" the silly fairy thing exclaimed suddenly. "Thank goodness. I thought that I was lost. It happens sometimes in such a gigantic place."

I stared at the room that we were in now. It didn't, most reassuringly, have any inhabitants, which I was extremely glad to find. There were still the shelves of books from floor to ceiling—evidently there was no shortage of them—but it looked a little more realistic for a disguised library. In the middle of the room, there was yet another glassy table, an exact imitation of the one that we'd seen earlier, and a regular brown desk next to it with a black swivel chair. It was perfectly ordinary, and it didn't have any potentially dangerous vials or potions. I was considerably relieved. But the air was still filled with the electrical magic charge, and my hands felt like they were on fire. I looked down and realized that I was covered with silver sparkles. And there were more floating down as well. I thought, *Oh great, a silver sparkle blizzard! What next?*

"Well, so what are we supposed to be doing here, exactly?!" Jenny demanded. "This place is, like, so wrong! I don't *want* to see fairies! I want to get the potion that we need, give them our wildlife report, and then be out of here!"

"Be patient," the silly fairy thing reprimanded her, giving her and the dragon a sudden contemptuous look. "I have a spell to perform over here!"

"Clearly you do," I put in.

She did some dancing and whizzing stuff in the air and then performed what I thought must be a summoning spell. It was tiresome, passionate, and extremely long and drawn out.

Eventually, though, the most annoying spell ended and a misty figure began to emerge from behind the wooden library desk. A sudden gust of wind knocked over some of the stuff that was on the desk, including a ruffly pen stand and a potion book, which rose into the air with stars and swirls coming out of it. I felt dazed. What in the world had I gotten myself into *this* time?

The mistiness suddenly cleared, and the figure became more visible. I gasped and took a step back.

"The witchy lady?!" I yelled.

Twenty Five

The Dragon Eradication Potion

She looked just as surprised to see me as I was to see her. Her face lit up for a second, and I began to think that she might not be as crazy as I had previously thought she was.

"Zoey!" she exclaimed. "I never thought that you'd be here!"

"Well, I am," I replied, "and I need the potion for Allie. Plus, we have some…um…*wildlife reports* that we'd like to give."

"Come right in," she said, gesturing to…um…was it the *wall*?! "I have a lab here for you guys to see. We were just creating the potion."

"But you're from like two hundred years in the past," I countered. "How did you get here?"

"Because once you read in that book that the potion you needed was here, I came to help them concoct the correct one for you to use," she explained.

"But how did you get here? You *definitely* didn't come the same way that we did, because……" My voice trailed off. I had been about to tell her that her age would prevent her from coming our way, but that was really rude.

"Oh, I have my ways," she responded, like Mary Poppins. She pointed to the wall behind her and a doorway appeared. She led us through it.

The room on the other side of the door was like some kind of age-advanced laboratory. Vials and test tubes of bubbling, steaming potions were everywhere on glassy tables, and screens that looked like hologram generators or touch-screen holograms covered all of the walls. There was nobody in there.

"Where is Allie's potion?" I demanded impatiently.

"Patience! It's currently in the process of being perfected...or, rather, being *refrigerated*," she answered.

I shook my head. "What does *refrigeration* have to do with any of this?"

"It has to go through a complex refrigeration, molding, redistillation, crystallization and melting process. Also, there's an alternating cycle. After each refrigeration—there are ten of them—it has to be sprinkled with a powder for reverse thermodynamic trajectory incantation—"

"Um, thanks for telling me, but I don't really need to know a whole lot of information about reverse thermo-blah blah blah...or whatever it is that you were saying," I mumbled with about as much politeness as I could muster.

"Point duly noted. Now, since the potion will take quite a bit of precious, ever-so-precious time to complete, you will be staying overnight—"

"Wait. We're staying overnight?" Jenny interrupted sharply. "Because for all I know, my mom has called the police, and they might even be combing the country for me now! I have to get *home*!" she cried with a renewed sense of panic. "And besides, can't you go into the time warp? My spells aren't strong enough for me to do that, but *you* can!"

"The potion won't work in time warp since the refrigeration won't be effective; it will be locked in a single moment in time," the witch responded as we stared at her in utter disbelief.

"So I guess we'll be staying here through nightfall," I gave in. "It's already past ten anyway. Sunset should be just beginning."

"So you remembered the thing about Pluto!" Jenny smiled with unmistakable pleasure.

✳ ✳ ✳

About an hour later, we were ushered into a magically generated bedroom space. It was classically styled, with bright white walls, and had an adjoining bathroom.

I had absolutely no trouble sleeping in that room, partially from exhaustion. It was really comfy, and the comforter was soft and fluffy. I was dreaming that I was in Fluffland, sleeping in fluffy clouds that felt like cotton, with Velvet on my lap, when at around three o'clock in the morning, all of a sudden…

THUD!

I had fallen off the bed, and I had some cold, sticky substance all over me. And yes, of course, as usual, naturally, I screamed.

Jenny sat bolt upright and threw off her comforter when she heard me. "*WHAT JUST HAPPENED?*" she shrieked.

I slowly opened my eyes, and I felt most disapproving about the present situation. It seemed as if, somehow, without any incantations, chanting, or spells, my bed had turned itself into *apple juice*! I was absolutely appalled!

"What in the—"

But before Jenny could finish her sentence, an even louder crashing sound came from one of the laboratories on the east wing of the building. I sat up, whistled a cleansing spell onto myself, and screeched at Jenny, "Let's go!"

We blindly dashed down to the foyer to where we thought the lab must be, along hundreds of narrow book corridors. At the end of one of them, there was a locked door leading to where we thought the sounds must be coming from. *Seriously*, I thought, *What's the use of locking doors if anybody can use magic to open them?*

Jenny whispered something and the door shot open. The room was fully lighted in spite of the ungodly hour, and at least thirty to forty miniature outrageous fairy things swarmed around what looked like a broken vial and potion. My face went white.

"Allie's potion!"

I dropped to the floor on my knees and began frantically searching for a trace of the seeping potion. The mob of fairies parted for me.

I retrieved a few drops and put them back into the vial, relieved. Then I noticed that some of the fairy creatures (I really hate them) were staring at me strangely.

I had the sudden urge to grab a fairy by its ankles and hang it on a clothesline. But the Witchy Council, or whoever all of these random witches and wizards were, certainly would *not* approve, so I decided to resolve the situation in the nicest way possible.

"Hey, what's the problem with what I'm doing?" I asked, corking the vial and standing up again. "It's *my* potion, isn't it?"

"No, it's not," a silly fairy thing in a pink dress with matching hair and shoes contradicted. "That potion was poisonous!"

I shook my head. "You guys have got to be kidding me! Please, *please* don't tell me that you make *poisonous potions* in this place!" I cried, not sure why I cared so much about the honesty of a few random witches that I didn't even know.

"It's not poisonous for you. It's poisonous for the dragons," another silly fairy thing with a purple dress whose name was probably *Beetrootica Vegetablifus* or some other such ridiculous nonsense explained. "They're using it to wipe out all of the dragons in the forest so that it will be safer to go through. Then every witch can come to the witchy HQ."

"But the dragons are perfectly innocent!" I shouted deliberately. "I promise! I can prove it to you! Really! See, I have a tame one right here!"

I produced the baby dragon, which skittered across my open palm. "It's cute, isn't it?" I asked innocently. Most of the fairies were slowly backing away from the poor reptile. Half of them had removed themselves to all the way across the room.

"It's dangerous," one of them said.

"But it's not!" I protested. "Can't you guys see that? I mean, what can it do to you?!"

"If you are talking about enchanting us and possibly killing us, then I should inform you that enchanting and killing a person *does*, in fact, amount to chargeable murder!" another silly fairy thing squealed in an unnecessarily frightened tone.

I rolled my eyes at them. "Well, if that's what you think," I muttered, "then stay quiet until tomorrow morning!"

"OK," the fairies chorused surprisingly obediently. "But we know that it's dangerous. It will probably enchant you while you're asleep."

Jenny stuck her tongue out at them, gathered up the vial, and then turned and followed me out of the room.

Twenty Six

Undue Surprises

I woke up exhausted the next morning and found myself quite literally swimming in apple juice. Annoyed, I went to most unnecessary lengths and enchanted the bed. It was very angry with me and followed me out of the room.

After freshening up, I met a bunch of equally tired fairies and witches in the dining hall. They stared at me with their mouths incredibly wide open as the bed comfortably seated itself onto an elaborate, gold-plated chair.

I shrugged. "It was mad at me for enchanting it. It followed me here."

"That's OK," one of the witches assured me. "Once the chair turns itself into shaving/whipped cream, that idiotic bed will learn."

Most unfortunately, though, the magic, as usual, acted upon me first. While helping myself to sweetened pancakes, I fell into a huge mess of something white, soft, swirly, and altogether extremely sticky. I couldn't imagine how these witches could actually manage to live all their lives in this place! So I calmly enchanted the chair, took away its ability to think and feel, and went on with my breakfast.

After breakfast, one of the witches showed us into a laboratory on the third floor. Apparently, that was where the potion was being made. Allie's potion was neon pink and blue, just like her hair. Then there were what looked like a whole lot of translucent, metal-substance tubes transporting some kind of bubbling liquid into the vial. It looked exciting.

There was a doorway on the other side of the room. I wondered what was behind it. When the witchy lady and Jenny weren't looking, I ducked my way around some witchy glass contraptions and advanced toward it. It said:

DRAGON ERADICATION POTION FACILITY

Oh no! So this was where the potion was being manufactured! I'd have to get into there and stop it somehow. I stared at the closed door and wondered if they had already tried it out on some dragons in the forest. I hoped not. For all I knew, the dragons were probably from the Cretaceous period or something like that......brought here by that evil wizard scientist. I didn't really like the idea of the poor dragons being wiped out by a violent meteorite, but it was history. They were probably quite miserable by now anyway in this strange desolate forest.

Suddenly, I heard some commotion on the other side of the hallway. Evidently, I had been missed already. I dashed back to where everybody else was, making a mental note of where this laboratory was located. Then I pushed a button on a TSH and the door swung open.

The rest of the morning was very boring. There was nothing much that we were allowed to do, and it was incredibly frustrating. Eventually though, once I had begged enough, one of the witches allowed us to explore a new lab facility in the northern wing of the building, providing that we didn't touch anything in there.

It looked extremely interesting to me. My attention was drawn to a test tube stand. The test tube held some kind of green, bubbling liquid. Breaking the rules, I snatched it. My curiosity overwhelmed me, and I picked up a small, gray, rock-like thing to drop into the test tube. Based on what I knew (which wasn't much), the rock-like thing was solidified lithium, which reacts violently to water. But I didn't think of the consequences. I just plopped it in.

I held my breath as the liquid bubbled and buckled as the two...or maybe even more...chemicals reacted with each other. Nothing much happened, so I felt encouraged and looked for something else to drop in.

Now, don't think that I wanted to mess up their witchy experiments, because I most definitely did not want to do so. I thought that I could clean up after myself using magic if anything became too messy, and thankfully, with the second element that I dropped in, nothing did become too messy.

The third "rock" variety, though, made the liquid in the test tube change color dramatically. It went from light, translucent green to red, yellow, and then purple, and alternated again. This had happened before on some cool science-y TV shows that I'd watched, but never in real life. I couldn't tell if the reaction was due to some witchy aspect of science or if it was just because of regular chemistry, but I did know that it looked amazing! I sniffed it, though well aware of poisonous gases, but it smelled like *raspberry perfume*!

Now, I began to get so excited that I played with any and every substance that I could find in the lab. I dropped in some lemon-and-orange-scented liquid from an eyedropper, and it turned the substance deep purple and kept it at the shade. I dropped in some liquid from yet another test tube and turned the substance orange. I had absolutely no idea what I was playing around with—it could have been deadly, for all that I knew—but I felt intrigued and also extremely lacking in common sense, for the time being at least. Jenny, too, was experimenting with the substances along with me now. At first she had protested endlessly about it, but after witnessing the unique color-changing abilities of some of the chemicals, she simply could not resist joining in. I didn't blame her at all.

The tenth thing that I dropped in, though, created a chemical reaction so violent that it knocked over the vial and bubbled almost to the point that it scraped the ceiling. I watched it, aghast. What had I done *this* time? I seemed to be walking into trouble everywhere that I went!

Once the substance stopped bubbling and fell from the ceiling, like a hurricane or, more aptly, an avalanche, it swept away everything in its most unfortunate path—that is, everything on the lab table. It knocked over jars of solidified xenon, magnesium, boron, fluorine, selenium, silicon, and hundreds of other unheard-of, potentially poisonous, or even deadly periodic table elements.

Jenny gasped. Her hands flew to her mouth. She began to furiously chant cleansing, purifying, and sweeping spells, but it didn't have any effect on the raging liquid tornado. This reassured me, though. If the spells had zero effect on the chemicals, then that meant that they must be weaker-magic-spell-defying potions...or something in that category.

Suddenly, the door burst open and a very angry-looking silly fairy thing whizzed in.

"What are you two doing?!" she demanded angrily.

"S-sorry," I apologized. "We'll clean it up. It's, um, just a little matter of a chemical reaction."

"*A little matter of a chemical reaction,*" the silly fairy thing mimicked sarcastically. "Of course not! What you just did has caused what is known as a *magical mishap,* and now we will have to clean up after you! I hereby forbid you two troublemakers from going in any more of the laboratories without prior permission, effective immediately!"

"Wait! Who told you that we never asked permission?!" I cried, but the silly fairy thing had gone already.

"*Now* look what you've done," Jenny seconded, after the silly fairy thing had left.

"It's not my fault!" I bluffed.

"You're lying!"

"I prefer the term, *subtly fibbing.*"

"Whatever it is that you were doing, we have to get the potion and leave!" Jenny yelled suddenly.

"But we have to persuade them to help the dragons first! *Remember?*" I reminded her.

"Sure, whatever," Jenny agreed.

"But..."

"But what?"

"I saw the room that they're manufacturing the potion in. We have to break into it at night and stop the circulation, because I'm pretty sure that the poison is pumped directly into the forest, if not by magic, then by some sort of a complicated piping system. Because I swear, a few drops of that poison could probably wipe out two to three entire dragon families!"

"I doubt it, but if it's being created in there, then we most certainly need to stop it," Jenny agreed.

I turned myself into a silly fairy thing, as ironic as it seems, and whizzed into the library downstairs. There seemed to be some sort of a fairy-witch, roundtable conference going on—in midair, which looked kind of funny. Witches, wizards, and fairies floated around in a seated position, with books and documents on their laps. Some of them leafed through witchy handbooks.

"Um, hi," I greeted one of the witches.

She looked up. "Hello, Zoey!"

"I'm sorry," I apologized

Her face took on a surprised look. "About what?" she asked.

"About, you know, making a gigantic mess in one of the laboratories," I answered.

"Oh, that's perfectly fine! I often do that. The fairies fix it for me. Who told you that it was such a disaster anyway?" She gestured for me to sit down in midair, and I hesitated and then did it. I was surprised to find that there seemed to be some kind of an invisible chair underneath me.

I turned my head insinuatingly toward one of the fairies. "She did!" I replied accusingly.

"*Rapunzel!* How many times have I told you to treat other witches and wizards with kindness?!" the witch chided.

"And now," she continued, "let us move on to more pressing issues. Zoey, Jenny, how are you two going to get home?"

"Just wash magic-strengthening spells over me so my magic is strong enough for teleportation back home. My magic wasn't previously strong enough for me to teleport myself here," Jenny responded immediately.

"I can get back home through time travel," I added.

"All right, then, that's settled. But the thing that we were wondering was…"

"WHAT WAS IT?! WHAT WAS IT?!" I cried, a little—I mean, a whole *lot*—too excitedly.

"Well, of course we wanted to know who wrote that book. And as you're obviously not going to tell us, we decided on a theory ourselves. All evidence suggests that your mom wrote it."

"You're the second person to tell me that, and I'm never going to believe it," I countered dryly.

Suddenly, there was a fluttering of small, glittery diamonds, and you-know-who materialized from the mist…with the book and the old book from the attic in her hand! She smiled down at me.

"Your mom wrote this," she revealed. "And what's more, we have irrefutable evidence to prove it!"

I shook my head. "It can't be! She'd have been famous by now," I said.

"She didn't tell anyone that she wrote it. The reason for that, of course, is that she either wanted to perform further experiments on it…or else, she's scared of the camera and the spotlight."

I burst out laughing.

"What's a camera?" one of the witches asked.

"It's an old-time version of a Capture 103 eyegram," another wizard answered her question. "Otherwise known as an old-time device that's used for, er, taking pictures," he added, straightening his tie.

"But how could you have figured it out?" I pressed, still confused.

"Easy! The new and highly sophisticated laser beam uncoverer, which discriminates luminiferous ether from the differentiated continuum of—" a studious-looking silly fairy thing in a pencil skirt and black stiletto heels began.

"OK, OK, I don't need to know all of this annoying, long, super-complicated stuff!" I exclaimed, awash in most severe boredom, which had actually resulted from that single little speech.

The silly fairy thing appeared to be terribly shocked and almost horrified. "But that's *basic vocabulary*!" she cried. "How could you not know…?"

"I feel that I simply must inform you that you are getting wildly off course here," a cute, stylish silly fairy thing wearing an aqua-colored ball gown reminded her.

"So, anyway," I interrupted, fearing that the argument between the two fairies would go on forever, "if my mom wrote it, then what does that mean? Do we win the Witchbel Prize?" I cried, my excitement level rising.

"Yes, after quite a bit of debate, you do, in fact, win the Witchbel Prize. That is, your mother does," a different witch put in.

"We're going to the Philippines resort and Queen Mackenzie Island!" I screeched.

"Zoey, we've been over this before," the head witch said gently.

"No, we haven't," I lied, staring at the other witches. "But seriously, what *is* the prize trip anyway?"

They all stared at me uneasily.

I stared back.

"Um," I urged, "so what is it?!"

Their expressions were tense and anxious. I wondered, and I wondered some more. Was it possible that they hadn't even *thought* of a prize trip? Then I could think of one myself! That would be fun!

Then one of the wizards cleared his throat. "Miss Zoey," he began in a proper voice, "Miss Zoey, the prize for the adult winner of the one and only Witchbel Prize is a trip for six to Hawaii."

I cheered, and I was pretty peeved when no one, not even the head witch, joined in with me.

"However," he continued, and I almost fainted with that lone word. "However, you may be rather—er—*surprised* with the prize for the child witch or wizard."

I braced myself.

He started grinning crazily. "The prize for the child witch of the winner for the Witchbel Prize is—a *free* scholarship to the most prestigious witch high school there is and will ever be in existence: *The Witchy Academy*!"

Twenty Seven

Major Destruction

I shook my head in a mixture of shock, annoyance, and yes, anger. *The Witchy Academy?* It was ridiculous! I could not even begin to imagine how horrible life would be over there. It was a most prestigious and well known boarding school, and as such was very difficult to get into—not that I had ever had any intention of getting into it anyway. It must be absolute *torture*! There wouldn't be any regular school subjects, I knew. It would all be witchy areas of education, designed to make a juvenile witch an amazing and exceedingly talented pioneer in the highly competitive field of witchy sophistication. Spells, potions, witchy dessert creations, Goth dress designing, complicated, possibly poisonous, new, advanced formulas…and reverse incantation. Subjects such as those were the only ones that we would be studying, and this was, ironically, a most distressing thought. I never thought that I'd actually *miss* studying algebra! I was appalled! Was *this* what my mom's smartness and winning the Witchbel Prize was going to get me? My face must have clearly portrayed what I was thinking because everyone—or should I say, *every witch*—around me was looking extremely sympathetic. This was just a "random" guess, but...did *they* know a whole lot about the witchiness-influenced terrors of such a school?

"It's OK," a witch assured me, seeing my panicked expression. "It'll be fun! You'll get to meet a lot of other nice witches your age and learn even more about spell techniques, potions, and the elements that a spell has to have to work—you'll even get to devise your own cool formulas! I myself went to The Witchy Academy when I was your age. I absolutely loved it!"

"Be quiet," I snapped.

"Oh, and by the way, *where* did you say you got your pet—um, *creature*—from?" Jenny asked, coming back in.

"You know what? I have no idea," I said. "Some spell went wrong and I must have actually performed a way more complicated conjuring incantation without knowing it. And Velvet is what I ended up with."

✳ ✳ ✳

I didn't sleep that night, and it wasn't because of thinking about the Witchbel Prize trip and school. I was thinking about breaking into the room and stopping the potion circulation to the forest.

You might think that I should have tried to patiently explain the situation to the fairies and witches, but I had already tried with the fairies, and it hadn't worked (I really hate those despicable creatures). This was even more risky now that I had been strictly forbidden from ever entering a laboratory, no matter for what purpose or reason, without prior permission. Again, I found myself wondering if doing so would permit them to violate my Eighth Amendment right...Could they inflict a cruel and unusual punishment on me, or would my parents have to bail me out using my allowance money? Now, though, I could probably think of worse punishments than having my makeup taken away from me, such as having Allie's potion taken away. That would be unimaginably horrible!

I could still hear stuff going on downstairs on the ground floor of the building. But eventually, around midnight, the commotion stopped, and I tiptoed out of my bed (most amazingly, it hadn't tortured me since we got mad at each other!). I debated with myself on whether or not to wake Jenny up. She was completely asleep, with Velvet on her feet. I decided not to, since it seemed much more exciting doing it by myself.

I knew where the laboratory was located now, so I got there pretty quickly. I tried the door and realized that it was locked. I had forgotten the spell that was used to unlock doors, so I had to go back to my room and get Jenny.

This was far easier said than done. Most unfortunately, on my way back to our magically generated bedroom, I met a very skeptical silly fairy thing. I had thought that everybody was in bed by now!

"Zoey! What in the witchy continuum are you doing at this ridiculous hour of night?" she demanded impatiently, clutching at her ponytail.

"Um, going to the bathroom," I lied sheepishly.

"Zoey, the bathroom—*your* bathroom, I mean— is right across from your room," she admonished severely.

"Oh, I forgot," I responded sarcastically. "Actually, I was here to check out how my sister's potion was getting along."

"Follow me then," she instructed suspiciously.

I was taken to the room where my potion was being made, which, incidentally, had a doorway that led directly to the dragon eradication potion room. The silly fairy thing smiled and whizzed over to the new age refrigerator, which had some extremely ingenious technology that allowed instant heating/cooling without electricity. It was really small and opened up with several compact compartments. Allie's reverse incantation potion was in the sixth and final compartment. It was swirly, neon pink and blue. There was equally swirly, cold steam coming out of it that was sparkly and sweet-smelling, like a mixture of fruity-scented Tressemé conditioner and blueberries. It looked yummy, but by now I definitely knew better than to try and eat any of it.

"The potion will be ready sooner than we expected; in fact, it will be ready tomorrow," she informed me. "So that you can go home soon."

I smiled at her. "I hope so," I agreed.

"Now, go to bed!" she exclaimed suddenly, her happy expression fading. "I still can't possibly imagine *why* this *particular* potion is so amazingly *interesting* to you!"

"Maybe because it smells like fruity-scented Tressemé conditioner mixed with blueberries and looks super yummy on a hot summer day," I replied dreamily, getting into the chemical transporter and pushing a few buttons.

"What is Tress-y-T-ress—whatever you called it?" she shouted after me.

I went back to my room and shook Jenny awake. "You need to get up! We're going to get rid of the dragon potion!"

"Ummmmmm…whatevs…" she murmured.

"No, I need you! I can't disable the locks!" I whispered urgently.

"Darn it! How is it that I always get stuck helping outrageous witches and wizards with outrageous problems?" she murmured in annoyance, following me to the lab.

She whispered something and focused intently on the door, and it slowly unlocked itself and swung open in response.

I was amazed by what I saw inside the room. Hundreds of narrow crystal-glass pumps were attached to vials containing the poisonous potion, which was a hideous dark green color. I blew my neon green bangs off of my forehead and felt relieved that they didn't look like *that.* The pumps were connected to each other and penetrated the glassy, glossy floor. I slid my four-inch wedge heels across the floor and knocked them into a pump. It shattered with a crash, spilling the potion across the floor in a sticky, gooey mess, and I looked up triumphantly.

"See? That's all that we have to do," I grinned. "Minus the crashing sounds, I mean. Soundproof the room with magic."

"This is fun!" Jenny exclaimed as she shattered another pump. "I have awesome destructive powers!"

We shattered pump after pump, and soon I began to worry that the pumps would shatter my shoes rather than my shoes shattering the pumps.

Eventually, though, we had finished destroying the circulation. Jenny smiled at the mess and snapped her fingers together twice. It disappeared immediately.

We were just going to exit the room when I heard another, louder sound coming from just outside. I held my breath. The door burst open suddenly, and I heard voices on the other side. Very angry voices.

"It's ZOEY! And JENNIFER! And they're DESTROY-ING the dragon eradication potion circulation pumps!"

Twenty Eight

"Wildlife Reports"

"No," I repeated to myself as a rage-stricken mob of annoying fairy things and witches stepped in.

"Miss Zoey, this is ridiculous," the proper wizard scolded in an extraordinarily calm voice. "What are you doing?"

"Sorry," I apologized, but not sheepishly. I simply handed him the baby dragon. He gasped.

"Oh my goodness! Miss Zoey, wherever did you get that from?"

"The forest; where else?" I replied, laughing nervously. "It's not meant to be here; we could tell. It let us pick it up and play with it, and it was nice to us! If it was brought into the forest for some random reason, then we need to get it back to where it should be!"

Soon, the entire place was absolutely buzzing with activity. I didn't even think of sleep; I couldn't. I followed the proper wizard into a spell laboratory and immediately felt a burning, tingling sensation fill my body. It was magic, and it was strong.

He didn't seem to notice that I was with him, so I calmly strutted out of the laboratory and headed to my room. I had most certainly gotten far more than my own fair share of excitement for one night. I needed to get a break.

I entertained myself by changing my hair into different colors and switching my makeup around in front of the mirror. Since I would be going to a witchy school next year, I could look as crazy as I wanted to—everyone else would probably look just as crazy too. I tried out hundreds of thousands of different color combinations and hairstyles, but none of them seemed to work. Pink and blue, like my little sister Allie. Red and black—Goth styling. Pink and purple. Green and blue. Brown with blond highlights, and quite a few more. I finally decided on light orange and deep berry, waist-length, totally straight hair with bangs. My lips were hot pink.

In fact, I was so amused with playing around with my hair that I didn't even notice Jenny and a whole lot of other fairies and witches screaming my name. I groaned and jumped into a chemical transporter. By the time that I got to the ground floor, everyone appeared to be completely and utterly exhausted.

"Getting your attention is like getting a—I mean, *the*—demented witchy scientist to adopt a baby foster teacup kitten and give it TLC," a silly fairy thing muttered, shaking her head. "And by the way, what did you do to your hair?"

"I changed it," I deadpanned.

"Obviously, you changed it," Jenny said, rolling her eyes. "You need to get your facts straight as well as your hair."

"But my hair *is* straight," I protested, confused.

Then the head witch stepped in. "Girls, stop arguing! Oh, the pointless and most meaningless arguments of my day! I get teary-eyed simply thinking about them," she murmured emotionally. "It was such fun. We would quarrel over the simplest things…who got the most cake, which witch was which—I was a quadruplet, you see—"

"Wait a minute. *You* couldn't remember your *own* name?! I mean, even if you're a quadruplet, that is pretty sad," Jenny interrupted.

"We are getting *really* off track here," I reminded them. "Like, seriously, guys, I don't even know what you were screaming my name for, and here we are discussing the long-lost arguments of your sentimental quadruplet sisters!"

"As usual," Jenny put in.

"We were calling your name out because of our baby dragon findings. We have just learned that they are a witchy version of some of the dinosaurs of the Triassic through Cretaceous periods," a soft voice from the doorway said.

I recognized that voice. It belonged to someone I knew, and I had absolutely no idea how they could possibly have gotten there.

I turned around and gasped. "*Mom*?!"

Twenty Nine

Back Home Again

She ran over to me. "It's you! Zoey!" she exclaimed, pushing across the mob of witches. "Finally, I got here!"

"But *how* did you get here?!" I asked, dazed.

"Magic," she replied. "After my findings about reverse incantation potions being concocted here, I decided to do some further experiments in order to figure out the specifics. I meant to allow you some time to get to the potion yourself, you see, to teach you a lesson."

I couldn't believe it. "But you did know it was dangerous, and you still let me go?"

"Of course not," she replied. "Had I ever known that it was so dangerous, I would never have let you go, even for the *incredibly important* purpose of teaching you a lesson. I didn't think that you could come to any harm with Cleopatra around. Apparently, I was mistaken. *Clearly.* So I had to step in and see if I could find you—and the potion." She glared at the head witch, but it wasn't really a real glare, just a joking one.

"Uuummm," I said slowly. I still wasn't completely sure what was going on. I clutched at the nearest desk, because fainting was a most definite possibility.

"I didn't want anyone to know about my little... er...*discovery* because I wanted to do further research on it, again, to figure out the specifics," Mom continued. "And I didn't want to call over a specialist either, because you weren't going to learn anything if someone else did all of the work for you. Cleopatra was actually giving me periodic updates on what was happening, so I knew that you had the correct book with the information you needed, and could go on to find the potion. I suppose my chief witchy friend here decided to give you a chance instead of making it easy and doing everything for you. I know Cleo very well, because she was actually the headmistress of the Witchy Academy when I went there."

"You went there." I felt dazed.

"Yes, I did, and it was lots of fun—" she began.

"You won the Witchbel Prize!" I squealed, mainly to cut her off from her little speech about how great the Witchy Academy supposedly was.

"*I did?*" she cried ecstatically.

"Yes!" I exclaimed. Then I remembered, and I sighed. "We're going to Hawaii. But now I have to go to The Witchy Academy."

"That's great!"

"No, it's not."

"But it is! You'll get a splendid witchy education!" Mom contradicted. "I went there too, and it's simply amazing!"

I rolled my eyes. "You don't say."

"The potion is ready," an oblivious voice announced from one of the laboratories.

"Let's go over there and see it." Mom led me over to the lab. The potion was out of the refrigeration sequence, and it was steaming and on a table. I miniaturized it and handed it to Mom.

"And now, it's time for us to go home," she told the rest of the witches and fairies.

"No! Not *now*," I protested.

"Yes, *now*," Mom responded. "We have to get home and change Allie back before anything else happens."

"But the dragons!" I cried, suddenly feeling panicky.

"We will take care of those," a different witch assured us. "We are currently working on getting them back to where they belong. We know the time period but not the place…However, we will soon retrieve the information."

I sighed. There was no getting out of it. We were going home, and we were going home right then.

"Um…bye," I said awkwardly to Jenny.

She didn't say anything. She just handed me her DSX. "That's for you," she told me. "I can easily get another one…somewhere over the rainbow, I guess. Actually in one of those tech stores. They're pretty cheap these days."

"OMG! This is, like, so awesome!" I squealed. "Thank you so much!"

"That's fine. You know, I was thinking, the reason that I gave you that DSX was so that once I get a new one, we can video chat. There's an app showing how to operate it," Jenny said. "So we can always talk to each other."

"That's nice," I replied sincerely. "And besides, I can come back here anyway, can't I, Mom?" I looked mischievously at her.

"That can be debated," she responded snappishly. "And now, please say bye, Zoey, so that we can *finally* get back home!"

"OK," I answered happily, although it was a little saddening to be leaving everyone.

I thanked every witch, wizard and even fairy in the room, and giving special thanks to Cleo for helping me so much. I waved goodbye rather sadly as Mom started chanting the time travel spell softly. Cleo, Jenny, and the rest waved back. I promised myself to visit them at *least* one more time, whether or not my mother approved of it.

And in a few minutes, we were spiraling home, past millions of nebulae and galaxies. It felt good to be home again. I felt like I was in a different world completely…and I was.

Dad was at work, so we went straight to my room, where Allie the bunny (but not for long! I hoped) was contentedly chewing on the rubber base of my favorite hot pink lava lamp. I gasped.

"*Allie! You despicable little monster!*" I yelled angrily.

Allie dropped the lava lamp, and it crashed into a million pieces on the floor as some kind of fluorescent liquid oozed out of it. I had always wanted to know what was in those beautiful, stunning, absolutely *gorgeous* lava lamps, and now I did know…but it would have been just a *bit* better if I could have been enlightened in a…um…more *subtle* manner.

Mom quickly dropped a little bit of the potion onto Allie's cute, fluffy bunny nose, and then all went black. The color of the walls and the temperature in the room shifted severely. When I could see again, there was no more baby bunny rabbit. Instead, it was Allie, standing there happily and looking immensely relieved. I just ran over and hugged her. My aggravating little sister was back.

"Zoey!" she exclaimed. "I'm so glad that I'm not a bun-bun-bunny anymore! It was like SO boring, and SO stupid, so I thought that I had to—"

And I stood there, smiling and grinning like a maniac, and listening to her yammering on and on about all sorts of ridiculous things she did in the house to ease her boredom, and not saying a word. My perseverance and courage, along with the help and total awesomeness of tons of friends, had finally paid off, and here was my little sister back to normal again. It was the best feeling in the world.

Made in the USA
Columbia, SC
10 November 2017